RENDEZVOUS
IN VENICE

PHILIPPE BEAUSSANT

RENDEZVOUS
IN VENICE

Translated from the French by
Paul Buck and Catherine Petit

PUSHKIN PRESS
LONDON

First published in French
as *Le rendez-vous de Venise* in 2003
Original text © Librairie Arthème Fayard, 2003

Translation copyright
© Paul Buck & Catherine Petit 2005
Special thanks to Sophie Lewis

This edition first published in 2005 by
Pushkin Press
12 Chester Terrace
London NW1 4ND

British Library Cataloguing in Publication Data:
A catalogue record for this book is available
from the British Library

ISBN 1 901285 55 3

Cover: *Venice, The Piazzetta with the Doge Marrying the Sea*
by Joseph Mallord William Turner
© Tate London 2004
Frontispiece: Philippe Beaussant
© Ulf Andersen Gamma

Set in 10.5 on 13.5 Monotype Baskerville
and printed in Britain
by Blacketts Limited, Epping, Essex

ii institut français

This book is supported by the French Ministry for
Foreign Affairs, as part of the Burgess Programme
headed for the French Embassy in London
by the *Institut Français du Royaume-Uni*

PART ONE

THE PAGES SLIP WHEN the notebook is bent slightly. They flick beneath the thumb far too quickly, with a soft shiver of paper. There is no time to read and yet words, bits of sentences, ends of lines jump out, as they say. If there were time, it would be interesting to write them all out one after another, to make a collection in the style of Raymond Queneau: what jumps at you from a book not read.

I wanted to stop a page with my thumb. Too late. It was gone. *I will never return to Venice* ... A finger stuck between the leaves. Eyes, lips, head stalled too. *Venice. never. return. never. Venice.* Incredible ...

What was incredible was that these words had been written by my Uncle Charles's own hand. Under my thumb, that inimitable spidering was him. Letters hardly shaken with age. Precise, regular, scrupulous, minute. And when I again flicked through the pages to find the sentence that had stopped me, it was his voice I heard colouring the words and fragments of lines I caught in passing. High-pitched, a touch nasal, and fine like his closely-written pages. *An angel painted by Bellini* ... *Am I or am I not capable of* ... *I looked over her shoulder* ...

My Uncle Charles never said *I*. When he used to pronounce that tiny syllable, it was not to say *me*. His *I* faded instantly behind something to do, like a stream trickling away under the bush that it nourishes and, in fact, gave life. "I'm going to write to Professor Lambrini." The *I* disappeared, Professor Lambrini filled the space. "I don't believe it, it really is a drawing by Il Guercino." The *I* vanished behind an angel roughly sketched three centuries ago on a scrap of paper. More recently, during his illness, when I entered his library and found him in his armchair, a blanket over his legs, the white scarf he was never without as always around his neck, his jug of water close at hand on the table covered with books, his old pipe in the Chinese ashtray though he no longer smoked, and said to him, "Good morning, uncle, how are you feeling today?", the answer blew aside the *I* even before we started talking about him. "My dear Pierre, we have a little mystery to solve today. I have just read that the drawing by Palma Vecchio we were talking about yesterday... " And there, in this little notebook that I'd just found by chance among his papers, during the brief moment when the pages had slipped under my thumb, *I* had jumped out, and more than that, an *I* tinged with regret, which allowed through something like an emotion. *I will never return to Venice ...* Incredible ...

The notebook in itself was strange and had surprised me straight away. I knew my uncle's papers. For years I had checked, shifted, transported, sorted, tidied, indexed, catalogued in bundles, piles, mountains of documents, notes and files. His entire life's work had been left to me, along with his table, his library, his filing cabinets, thousands of letters from distinguished museum curators and university professors from all over the world. His habits I knew well too, and, besides, they made my task much easier. He only wrote in large bound notebooks he bought in England, or on large sheets, English size too, of beautiful, strong paper, smooth and soft. If by chance he made a note unexpectedly, he would copy it down that night onto one of his sheets of paper and give it to me to file away.

"Pierre, will you please put this in the folder, 'Van Dyck in Genoa', and make a note to add to the file of the Lord Stockville Collection. Thank you, Pierre." The dimensions of the paper, the colours of the folders, the titles of the labels. Order, method, habits. Mania, if you like. Some, watching him work, would perhaps have said: this man is an old crack-pot. And, of me, his nephew, his secretary, his assistant, his irreplaceable: he is the assistant crack-pot.

My Uncle Charles was a man of order. At every moment in his life, he was as he was going to be at the moment of his death. Perhaps we should say that the way he died had to be like a concentrate of what he had been in all matters. I suppose it is like that with all deaths. Only then do we reveal the truth of the person we have been. If at this moment we seem to be different, if fear, suffering, what one calls agony, seem to transform us at the moment of the final passing, it is perhaps only that we had concealed what we were, or that we had concealed it from ourselves, and didn't know it.

It was the night-nurse, the one I had met several times when I came late in the evening to pay a brief visit to the clinic, who told me next day the story of his last fifteen minutes. His body had already been taken from the room, as is normal in those public places which are built for death and where, nevertheless, one mustn't see it. I had returned to collect some of uncle's belongings, for I was his sole surviving kin. I encountered the young white-clad woman in the corridor and she recognized me. This young blond nurse had grown attached to him, probably because, beneath his stern shell, he was friendly and considerate, and perhaps also because of me, for it is natural to be interested in someone when others show them consideration. I feel sorry for those people who are alone in life, for there is no reason why a stranger should be interested in those in whom no-one else is.

During his last few days, she allowed me to stay a bit longer than the time prescribed for authorised visits. She asked me to leave the room when she was taking care of him, then reopened the door and the three of us exchanged a few words, like a kind of family. I remember that last night with my uncle exactly, as if my memory, more attentive than I, had one of those premonitions which makes us retain all the details of the moments it had already guessed would never come back again. That evening, after the young woman had left, my uncle said, with the slight half-smile he used to make more with his eyes than his mouth when he was about to offer a witticism:

"Tell me, Pierre. Please explain why nurses so often seem prettier than the average young women one meets in the street?"

These small dramatic turns that my uncle, so serious and severe, sometimes sprang on me, always took me by surprise. Never had I imagined he could look at young women in the street. Never.

"Do you think so?"

"Yes. I've noticed it … "

I reflected on the consequences of such a general comment and, of course, I looked for arguments to challenge him, without trying too hard though, for my uncle never opened his mouth without having studied every aspect of a problem at length. Thus, when he spoke, what he said was quite clear. In reality, in his mind, the problem was already resolved. He never improvised, he didn't fumble about, like most of us. His voice was clear and precise, his sentences had the constructed, studied, definitive authority of printed formulae. They were fashioned like written lectures. They were already that in his head. Sometimes I tell myself that if I too think and speak in a slightly formal manner, it's because I've done nothing else for fifteen years but take care of him, his affairs, and his writings.

"Yes, I've noticed it since I've been here and I think I've found the explanation."

As I said, my uncle never asked a question without already having the answer. And so he seemed infallible.

"It comes from the fact their clothes are totally impersonal. So one only looks at their faces, and, without thinking, looks there for all possible marks of grace. As they take care of you, and you are grateful for it, and tell them so, their smile takes on a charm it perhaps wouldn't have if one saw it on a woman wearing a colourful dress, as that would distract us from looking at her."

When uncle had an idea, he didn't stray from it. He dug deep, picking out all the consequences.

"Look at the Flemish portraits … "

Besides, the consequences almost always took their bearings from the world of painting.

"All those women, young and old, with the same white ruff pinned at their necks, the same black dress without ornament, the same peaked veil on their foreheads. How their faces become individual when their dress is not … You see, Pierre, that is why the Dutch became such great portraitists … "

That is why for fifteen years I have been such a faithful and attentive disciple to my uncle. At any moment, an everyday event could become a lesson in History of Art.

"They had nothing else to paint. No Virgin surrounded by Saints, no ancient heroes, nothing. Black dresses and faces. Nothing for the imagination. Only eyes, wrinkles, cheeks, mouths. Art fixes on faces. Or else a timid ray of sunshine in a dining room corner, or a reflection on a crystal glass between two apples, peaches, a bunch of grapes and a tulip. Do you know, Pierre, I'd gladly say that art is all the greater when we restrict its freedom to blossom."

And there went my uncle, finding himself once more in the only universe which was real to him. (Uncle would have said, which could be real to him. He used the subjunctive in the most ordinary conversations. It was pure joy to hear him address one of his female students at the Art Institute: "Miss, it would be advisable if you 'were' to pay more attention to chronology"). The only universe that could be real for him was painting. I should say the universe where life condensed and concentrated so as to become a stronger, fuller reality. Thus the honest Dutch women painted by Gerard ter Borch or Emanuel de Witte became to him witnesses of a universal truth, and the blond nurse who treated him every evening in that sad enamel-painted room wore an echo of that truth in her smile.

Such was my last conversation with my Uncle Charles: thoughts about a smile. It was late. I left, wishing him a good night. What followed I learnt the next day from the young woman.

As with every evening, she had come to administer the final treatment for the day and to replace the bottle in uncle's drip. When she wanted to switch off the lamp, he had asked in his dry voice, in the solemn and convoluted sentences of which he was so fond, for permission to read a few more pages of the book he was holding. She repeated his words to me with—should I say, a form of devotion? Yes, that was it. As if she could have seen in the way he was looking at her, the transformation of her own smile into a work of art, that she then gave back to him.

"I pray you, Miss. See for yourself. I only have three pages left. I don't like to go to sleep without finishing my chapter. It is discourteous to the author who took pains to conclude it."

I can just imagine him. He must have lowered his glasses to the tip of his nose, his eyes directed at her over the lenses, his hands on the sheets, one holding the book, the index

12

of the other marking the page. And, as my uncle was an orderly man in all things, including the nature of things, and it was in the nature of things that a young nurse should give orders to an elderly patient, even to a member of the Institute, his face must have borne the expression of a good little boy, slightly shy, who asks his teacher very politely for permission to go out and play.

"Three pages you say? Very well, but not one page more, Professor. Promise me?"

She was laughing sweetly, playing along with him now, and taking the tone of a school mistress by lowering her voice and pointing her finger.

"Furthermore, I'll be back in a quarter-of-an-hour to see if you're an obedient patient."

It was his turn to smile, as he replied with his characteristic inarguable logic.

"Why should I begin a new chapter that I would have to abandon in the middle to obey you?"

She had left. She had closed the door gently, had visited a few other patients less well-behaved and less sprightly than he in the neighbouring rooms, and then, as she had promised, she had returned precisely a quarter-of-an-hour later to turn off the light. The book was closed on the night table, the glasses placed carefully on top. And he was dead.

To die without having finished his chapter, never. That was my Uncle Charles.

That is the reason why, even before opening it, I had been surprised by that little notebook. Among my old uncle's files, it had seemed lost, as incongruous as a mushroom grown by itself in the space of one night in the middle of a neatly-mown English lawn. Where did it come from? What was it doing there? To whom did it belong? For, at first, I hadn't even imagined it could be his, so out of keeping was its green card cover among my uncle's endless papers. I was even more astonished to discover lines written in his own hand as I flicked the pages under my finger. Without giving it much thought, I expected the writing of a stranger, a student, or a colleague. Not at all. Those minute characters carefully drawn, the double *l* like a dragonfly, the scroll of the *j*, the *t* crossed with something like an arrow, and between the words those white spaces measured like breaths. It was certainly him. *I will never return to Venice.* My wonder grew as I turned the pages, without really reading, my thought a prisoner to that incredible sentence. The sound of my uncle's voice took hold of those words I'd caught in passing and then of others, becoming ever more present. *Scuola di San Rocco, San Zaccharia, Rezzonico, Carpaccio,* all proper nouns, their capitals carefully embellished, drew my eye and took me back at each sound to Venice. The voice began to solicit other sounds: the lapping of water, a bell, Italian sounds, then, more precisely, the little taps of Uncle Charles' walking stick, muffled suddenly as he took the first wooden step of the Ponte dell'Accademia. I was not reading, I was wandering between words, plucking them out haphazardly. *Tiepolo, his element is air.* Well put, uncle. Just like you. I already knew that sentence and in my memory, I heard him continue: "We think it is water, the lagoon, but no, it's air. Characters in space, that's the subject of his paintings. Armide and Esther are only pretexts … " And hearing my uncle like this, present to my ear, as if he hadn't died five years before, made me understand why I went on browsing through that strange notebook, without reading it. As if a shyness, a discretion, a restraint were dissuading me. A knock at the door. It opens. "Oh, sorry… excuse me, I … " I laughed to myself, hearing him say: "Pierre, could you please place this little notebook in the file of … Thank you, Pierre." Only after I finished laughing did I start to read at random on the open page.

… her eyes lowered towards the green water and the objects floating on its surface. She doesn't look round, entirely absorbed in her thoughts, or in contemplation of some bits of wood or paper drifting to and fro with the lapping of the canal …

For a second I thought I glimpsed a Canaletto tableau showing a dreamy Venice with green waters and reflections carefully smoothed out with little brush strokes, but in which the unexpected silhouette of a woman would stand in the foreground. I looked up. Which painting? Which museum? Which collection? There are never any characters in the foreground of a Canaletto. Strange … Intrigued, I went on with my reading and found that it was nothing to do with a painting, and that my uncle was not only saying *I*, but also *me*.

She is waiting for me. And I, from the bridge, I watch her waiting for me. I am still recovering from a bad night in the train. It is cold, that damp cold which is colder than cold. That woolly mist of Venice in the winter penetrates me. I stay up there. From the bridge I contemplate the most beautiful sight a man can imagine, especially if, like me, he is moving towards what one calls 'maturity': an attractive young woman, not only attractive but desirable, tender and sweet, who is waiting for him. She seems so absorbed in her waiting that she pays no attention to anything around her, not even to me, already there and looking at her. And I delay the moment when I will take her in my arms so I can savour a while longer this strange pleasure of looking at her waiting for me.

Oh … uncle …

This pleasure is so intense, the emotion it provokes in me so strong, that it is that moment I remember after so many years and not our embrace. I should be ashamed. I am ashamed. How did I get down? Did I call her? Did I rush down the stairs? Did she look up? Was it she who saw me first or did I make the first move? I would like to be sure I shouted from the bridge, I would like to be sure that it was I who made the first move. I don't remember any longer and that makes me feel ashamed.

My astonishment was such that I didn't notice at first that below the words I'd just read were those I was looking for. It took me a few seconds to recognize them.

I shall never return to Venice. The places I liked are becoming hazy in my memory. They lose their outlines, as San Giorgio Maggiore does in October in the evening light. Could it be that the Venice of my memories ceased to be completely real a long time ago? Its palaces and campaniles doubtless already look like those painted by Turner. Like him I invent them, I reconstruct them with a more fluid and vaporous material, I colour them without meaning to, to make them look slightly more like the happiness I felt in contemplating them. Perhaps it is less them I remember and more the happiness. But what about Judith?

I carried on deciphering those pages in which everything betrayed my uncle's hand. In each letter, in each stroke, in each curve, even in each space, he was so fully alive, so present through those familiar signs that it was as if he spoke to me. I could hear what I was reading. I could hear him with his own voice, and it was belatedly that I suddenly realized it no longer reached me, as if fallen silent. What I had beneath my eyes had ceased, I don't know when, a moment earlier, to be accompanied by his presence. What I was reading had been written by his hand, but he was no longer there.

I lifted my head, surprised by this silence that had taken place within me.

I read the top of the page again:

… I, already there and looking at her. And I delay the moment when I will take her in my arms so I can savour …

Impossible. My uncle couldn't have written that. The letters were his, but not the words.

I looked around me at the austere office, the books, the table with its ashtray and tobacco jar. Impossible. I forced uncle to speak in my head. "Pierre, would you be kind enough to put this note in the 'Van Dyck in Genoa' file. Thank you, Pierre." Between the sound of that voice and what I'd just read, there was no possible connection. Was it I who had silenced him, as if the link between what I had under my eyes and his presence had to be severed?

What I read was not him. He had transcribed someone else's text. It was a copy. *I* was not him. Besides, Uncle Charles never said *I*. And as for Turner: as far as I knew he was never interested in that English painter who saw Venice through a blue and yellow mist. I knew the Venice of my uncle. How many times had we been there, him and me? Bellini, Carpaccio, Titian. But whose was this text, that he had gone to the trouble of copying into the strange little notebook? For what purpose? Why be interested in a man who arrives in Venice to meet a woman, as would many a *gallant* or lover since Alfred Musset and Georges Sand? There were no women in my uncle's life, no spouse, no daughter, no niece or cousin, no other family than me and old Mariette, his servant.

It was all my fault. Why hadn't I started reading at the first page, instead of opening it at random, as I had done? I'm sorry, dear uncle, for this lack of method, unworthy of one who would be your disciple.

Today my old aches are coming back to make me suffer. The weather is changing. I won't go out. There is no point in forcing myself, as I used to in the past, to walk a few steps to stretch my legs, to force my limbs to move and give a little ease to my rusty joints. I used to do that still, two or three years ago. I increased my suffering by sheer force of will, by walking twice round the pond, hand clutching the walking stick, sometimes going as far as the woods. I used to come back stiffer than when I'd left, so that I had to ask for help with the front steps, and felt humiliated for that act of will that was nothing but pride. Now I place my pride elsewhere, that's all. When September comes, I know what to expect and I am preparing myself so as to depend as little as possible on anyone. Like an adventurer ready for an emergency departure who keeps his bag under his bed with its biscuits and a first-aid kit, I arrange on this corner of the table some pipes and a tobacco jar, a few books and the blanket folded on the armchair. From time to time I add a book which springs to mind, for the day of the first attack. I'm getting ready to live in this corner, and economising my movements is the only way I've found to lessen my suffering and the need I could have of other people. I agree to people coming to talk to me, but I don't wish to be served.

Yes, there, that was really him. I recognized him in his gestures, movements, habits. Stiff, as he had always lived, even before the affliction of those rheumatisms which immobilised him every winter. Severe with himself as he was or pretended to be with his associates, intimidating with his pupils, and a little with me.

But why that sharp tone I didn't recognise?

Yesterday I made the most of these final moments when I can move without suffering too much. I searched my shelves for a few books to add to the pile on my table. My concern each year in this season, each day more absorbing, more haunting, is to think of everything. I know from experience it's always the book that's not there that I will need to read at the moment when Pierre will not be here to find it. But my table is already creaking with books. So why did I take out that book yesterday? I told myself: chance. What chance? I couldn't even remember owning that uninteresting work riddled with mistakes. I pulled it clumsily from its shelf and it fell. What happened then? I want to know. I don't believe in chance. I bent down to pick it up. Groaning with pain I made a terrible effort with my back and the joints of my legs and then I exclaimed loudly: 'Oh my God, Judith ... ' How could I have said those words, pronounced Judith's name before opening the book and

*finding the photograph concealed in it? I said: 'My God, Judith … '
and I know that the burst of pain didn't come solely from my back.
Slowly, holding onto the shelves of the bookcase, I hauled myself up and
went to sit down again. I had not yet opened the volume. I had not yet
seen Judith's face and I said: 'How can one be crippled? How can one
be an invalid? How can one be old?' with an anger that came not from
my pain but from a kind of disgust and hatred that I don't understand.
'How can one be old? Am I going gaga? I'm talking aloud … '*

Who was Judith, Uncle Charles? What are you saying
to me? What is the pain you talk about and yet can't say
if it comes from your body tortured by arthritis—or from
somewhere else? And why do you ask yourself that question,
if it's not to answer what you know perfectly well, that
doesn't come from your rheumatism?

My poor dear uncle, how could I have seen you so often,
talked with you, travelled with you from conferences to
exhibitions, had endless conversations with you in your
office or in trains taking us to Amsterdam or Munich, seen
you, looked you in the eyes and not once sensed that there
were such things you would say to yourself when you were
alone?

Who is this Judith whom you embrace in Venice? I'm
bewildered …

How can I imagine my austere old uncle with a woman?
I only ever saw him with old Mariette dressed in black, with
her blue apron and her hair in a bun, herself resolutely old-
fashioned, smiling sometimes, yes smiling, looking up from
her work or into the glass of the window she was busy wiping
and who, I knew, reminded my uncle of Françoise in *Swann's
Way*. How can I imagine Uncle Charles close to a woman?

Yet, of course, women were not absent from his thoughts.
He loved them. I know, I've seen it. When he started to talk
about them, he just couldn't stop. But they were always

painted women. He talked about them like a lover but, unlike a jealous lover, he gave the impression, while talking about his beloved (the beautiful Eleanor of Toledo, painted by Bronzino, or Giovanna Tornabuoni in the fresco of Sante Maria Novella) that he would have wished you to share his passion and that his dearest desire was for you to fall in love with her too. He would describe her as if she were alive, with the same detached, reserved tone he would have for a minor question of museology but with a sudden imperceptible inflexion, soft and solemn, which made me turn towards him, while his gaze caressed, with a half-smile, an image of a woman dreamt by Botticelli. And immediately that mute and motionless figure, fixed on canvas five centuries ago, seemed to be roused to a mysterious life, as if it could have been the memory of a familiar character that one had met the day before, had seen walking, gesturing, turning her head.

"Do you know, Pierre, that if you look at the portrait of Simonetta, in Chantilly, painted by Piero di Cosimo (for a long while attributed to Pollaiuolo, but that's a mistake …) you can hear her speak?"

My uncle only ever knew the details in things. Thus the image of the woman began to construct itself with the help of tiny and insignificant facts, elements from ordinary everyday life, little oddities and small defects that make up one's existence.

"Look at the mouth. Have a good look at her lips, Pierre. They are so perfectly drawn, with such marvellous precision that you know the sound of her voice. I can testify that, although she was from Genoa (always the imperfect subjunctive with which my uncle sharpened his sentences), she pronounced Italian with the delicious linguistic peculiarity one hears here in Venice. It is written on her mouth. Can you see?"

And my uncle, with the tip of his finger, traced the outline of an imaginary lip whose original was in Chantilly, or more precisely in the portrait of a woman dead five centuries ago, painted by a certain artist, or perhaps by another, Piero di Cosimo, or else Pollaiuolo, who was to know?

"You can hear how she recites the short love poems written for her by Lorenzo di Medici, exactly how she used to pronounce them. It's the relationship between the lower lip and the upper. Can you see?"

And while sketching the outline of a mouth in the air, Uncle Charles whispered, or rather, sang quietly, imitating the soft lisp that makes Venetian lips so attractive: *"O felici sospiri e degni pianti … "*

A kiss, dear uncle? How to imagine that? I can't imagine it. Today he imposed over my memory of him this incredible thought that he could know intimately the outline of a woman's lips, although I had never seen him close to one. He was aware of all the trappings of fashion, armholes, cut, cloth, pleats, tassels, slashes and knots. He knew their symbolic language and secret codes, as if he had lived intimately with the one whose portrait we were looking at, attending to her toilet, as one used in those days, as a faithful admirer or lute player, or else as a lover trysting with his beloved on a secret staircase (but how to imagine, without laughing, my dignified and respectable Uncle Charles unfastening the stays of one of Lucrezia di Medici's waiting maids, or kissing the neck of Tullia d'Aragon?). He knew all the movements, the hand language, tricks of gait. ("They change," he used to say, "with each generation.") He recited the old dates of five centuries ago as if leafing through his diary to find the date of a meeting.

"It happened, I think, on April the twenty-sixth … "

Then, after a second during which he concentrated, screwing up his eyes as we do when trying to recapture the exact chain of events:

"Yes, of course, the twenty-sixth, since … "

And he resumed:

"Did you know, Pierre, that that date, the twenty-sixth of April, seems to be marked by fate in Florence? On April twenty-sixth, Simonetta died. Guiliano di Medici died two years later to the very day, on April twenty-sixth 1478, by the knife of Francesco di Pazzi, in the chancel of Santa Maria dei Fiori, stabbed so many times and so furiously that his murderer severely wounded himself as he relentlessly struck at the body of the man he had already killed ten times over."

Uncle Charles recited like a book. When he told a story, his sentences took on in his mouth the ordering of finely written phrases, with subordinate clauses and imperfect subjunctives shining like highly-polished copper buttons. Listening to him, one had the feeling one was leafing through a book. On that day, I remember now, we had spent the afternoon at the Accademia. Coming out we had, as always, paused before Bellini's *Magdalene*, only for a moment, as one stops to smile at somebody one loves, when one meets her on the street. Uncle Charles had courtesy for masterpieces as he did for people. One didn't pass Bellini's *Magdalene* without a friendly word, in one's thoughts. Then we had dined at a small *trattoria* near the Campo San Stefano before walking back. At that point, Uncle could still get around without any pain. We crossed the small tangled canals of the San Maurizio and Sant'Angelo neighbourhood, with their tiny bridges, and my uncle leaned on his elbows on the railings of one of them. This was the time of day, I knew, when he let himself go a little, when his imagination wandered freely. He drew on his pipe, and the reflection of the water's undulations brought momentary flushes of light to his face, colouring the small puffs of smoke he spread around him with the pinkish gleam of night fall.

"Do you realize, Pierre, what Florence was like that year?"

A few seconds of silence, some curls of smoke, waves on the canal, and it was as if we had stepped aboard a gondola.

"Botticelli was twenty-five. Ghirlandaio was twenty. Filippino Lippi was nineteen. Leonardo da Vinci, eighteen. And their master, Lorenzo di Medici, was twenty too. What youth! Lorenzo discussed philosophy with Marsilio Ficino and composed sonnets for the beautiful Lucrezia Donati, who was then ... how old was she? Twenty-two or twenty-three. The world was very young, Pierre. Or rather, I think that in Florence it had begun to get younger. There are moments in history when everyone is young, and others which are only populated by old people, and when events begin to stutter and ramble. That year in Florence, a young woman arrived amid the youth of that world and the whole of Florence fell in love with her. Everybody. Lorenzo, his brother Guiliano, the whole court, the poor people in the streets, the shopkeepers, the old people, the musicians, the painters, the monks in their monasteries, everybody. She was sixteen and the world was doing everything it could to be like her. Don't you find that astonishing, Pierre? A sixteen year old girl who, without doing anything other than being who she is, beautiful, amiable, sweet, yes, that absolutely, gracious, clever, shapes a city, orders people's lives, leads the thought of painters and poets—simply by who she is. And you see, Pierre, what is most surprising is not her at all, it is what was born from all that."

Uncle had paused in the middle of his thought. He tapped his pipe three or four times on the iron rail of the small bridge. I knew that signal.

"A true masterpiece, I speak of those which will never die, which are forever a small treasure men have given to the world, a true masterpiece is a work which offers in its most beautiful form the most faithful image of the epoch of its birth."

And, after another second of silence:

"There are no exceptions."

I knew that when he had to say such a sentence, Uncle Charles would remove his pipe from his mouth and strike it on something to empty the ash: the ashtray, the railing or his hand if he couldn't find anything else nearby. It was his way of hammering out the words, while his voice didn't change in tone or volume. Two or three taps and I knew that the sentence so anticipated was to be remembered by heart.

"The epochs, Pierre, which don't find those means to transmit the strong and beautiful things they have, or which transmit them through ugliness (it happens) or derision (that happens too), are those which later, with the passing of time, are said not to be worth remembering or discussing. That too is without exception."

My uncle had paused again. We were looking at the last phosphorescence on the waters of the narrow canal and the perfect circle formed in the gloom by the small bridge and its reflection, a few dozen metres away from us. I remember uncle had told me on another evening that Venice was the only city in the world where every artifice was allowed in order to reach perfection. Elsewhere, he said, one distinguishes the lies clearly. In Venice, one could still see them, but one takes pleasure in pretending to believe them. The curve of the bridge and the inverted curve of its reflection, one real the other virtual, formed a perfect circle which was a illusion, but all the more pleasing for that knowledge. Then we spoke of Florence, where pretence is impossible. And I think that is precisely what my uncle meant to say. I could only guess at his smile in the semi-darkness when he resumed:

"You are wondering, my little Pierre, what is the link between what I'm saying and the gentle Simonetta Vespucci? I shall tell you. Or rather, not I but Botticelli. If I tell you that at the time when Simonetta turned up in Florence, the world was getting younger, it's not a figure of speech. I should have said more precisely that it was flourishing again. Do you understand the *Primavera?* "

We were there. Uncle Charles' thinking could make large loops. One thought he was wandering, had lost the thread, when suddenly one found oneself back on track, without knowing how.

"We have never known exactly what that painting represents. Who is that woman? What are the three Graces doing there? We know nothing about it. We don't know what that fat chubby-cheeked Zephyr is doing, blowing and stretching his arms towards a nymph who seems to be chewing parsley? And what about Mercury, who seems to be busy gathering apples? We have no idea. But that is not important, since the true subject of a painting is not what it tells, but what it shows. What the *Primavera* shows is simply springtime in Florence. And as it is perfectly beautiful, it is the image of that world's youth. But look carefully, Pierre. Consider all the paintings produced by Botticelli in his lifetime. All the women who appeared under his brush, Venus emerging from her shell, naked and beautiful, the Virgin with the pomegranate, the Virtues, Jethro's young daughters, all resemble each other. They look like sisters. Do you know why? Because they are all a dream of Simonetta.

He only ever painted her, or his memory of her. Were you aware, Pierre, that forty years after her death (she was twenty-three when she died), Botticelli asked to be buried at her feet, in the Ognissanti chapel? He is still there. Twenty-three year old. Guiliano di Medici loved her too, for six years, without once touching her. When she arrived in Genoa, she was sixteen. Her cousin Amerigo Vespucci was going to give his name to a whole continent that nobody had yet … "

Uncle Charles was recounting the history of the world through the gaze of a painted woman.

"A year after Simonetta's death, Guiliano competed in a big tournament, one of those celebrations of men and horses adored throughout Italy, where all the people in town watched in the square, at windows, on balconies, on rooftops. You've never been to Siena, Pierre? What a shame. The celebration of the Palio is perhaps the most vibrantly alive of those customs that remain today from the Renaissance. We have museums, we have preserved palaces and carved galleries that we love. We have paintings which are, for you and me, the most precious things in the world. But the living Quattrocento, full of movement, shouting its pleasure, its horses prancing, is in Siena on the day of the Palio; you can see still go to see it. On that day, on his horse caparisoned in velvet and gold, Guiliano di Medici brandished a banner on which had been written in French: *la Sans-pareille,* lady without equal, and on which Simonetta's face had been painted by Botticelli. A simple flag, for a sporting contest, painted by Botticelli. Can you imagine that? All of Florence's working population was there too, like today at the Palio, and it saw itself mirrored proudly in the sweetest woman and handsomest man. For that too needs to be said."

He tapped his pipe on the iron rail.

"When a people can no longer admire itself, it is lost."

Once again he fell silent, his eyes fixed like mine on the last gleam floating on the water beyond the circle of the bridge. He packed fresh tobacco into his extinguished pipe and resumed, without lighting up:

"Once again there are no exceptions. You see, Pierre, man can be measured by his capacity for beauty. That is why I told you I don't like derision. A man who forces himself to laugh, who vents his malice under cover of what one mistakenly calls humour, is a man who is not happy at heart. The same for a people. When people can only express themselves through derision (not mockery, that's not the same thing), that's because they are in pain and can't say anything more, can't paint or write or play without groaning like a deep rheumatism in an invalid."

The links of my uncle's thought were always fantastically logical. One might think he was wandering. But when he came back to the subject, one understood he had never left it, even when the link was made through a minute detail.

"Talking of Simonetta's portrait, in Chantilly, don't ask how long she needed to have her hair done, let alone give a thought for the coils of her blond locks, and forget the curl that undulates around her neck, which one always imagines as a necklace or a dainty tamed snake. Forget her small breasts, which are so ravishing, but so chaste that one cannot imagine thinking to caress them. And rightly, for the painter tells us through the ravishing modesty of his painting that Guiliano never did that. Forget all that. Look at her eye. She doesn't look straight ahead, but slightly higher. It is the only profile I know which has such a look. What do we all do, you, me, stupidly? We look straight ahead. Simonetta doesn't look straight ahead, but slightly higher. As if the truth of things and the beauty of the world were just a tiny bit higher than where we think they are. There are paintings where beautiful saints raise their eyes to the sky … "

Uncle laughed slightly.

"I mistrust them … There are also sweet Flemish madonnas who lower them with a charming timidity that touches my heart. But I feel like saying one word to them (nothing more, just one word: *ave*) so that they will hear me and I will be able to meet their eyes. Simonetta overwhelms me and even more for one doesn't know what she is looking at, far away, beyond the frame."

On her lips she had always the beginning of a smile. One could not know if, indeed, she was about to smile, or if she was only playing with a thought or an idea in her head, which would have caused that kind of inner joy. But the outline of her mouth had in itself the shape of the beginning of a smile, so people liked her without knowing why. As for myself, I learned later that the outline of her lips was in truth produced by the sweetness of her inner world and that her mouth had in reality been moulded since childhood by that happiness she carried within. For it is not given to everyone to display this miraculous agreement between their inner peace and their face. I know my dear Mariette well, for she has served me for so many years. She is a good and kind woman. But why can one read in her eyes, on her mouth, in the wrinkles of her cheekbones, only the mark of her endless demands, of her dissatisfaction, which comes from such insignificant things—the excessive butcher's bill, his tough meat, or the postman's late arrival? She forgives all for she is truly good and charitable, but nothing of this kindness shows in her features. I could never see the difference between the expression of a bad person and that of an unhappy person. The external signs are just the same. Are the wrinkles brought with age the same whether from unhappiness lengthening or continuing, or as inner bitterness becomes more pronounced? But what is the link on the face, between kindness and happiness? Did the barely drawn, barely suggested smile on Judith's lips signify at the same time that she was kind and that she was happy, and that she would never, whatever the circumstances, let misfortune take her?

Uncle Charles had a certain way of looking at people that had intrigued me for a long time. It used to happen at particular moments and always in the same circumstances. It was precisely the regularity of those situations and the strange expression on his attentive and smiling face which had attracted my attention. Later, allusions and half-sentences had gradually shown me what was happening in his mind. But it was much later, years later, that he confided in me with a shy smile what he used to call his 'little failing', his 'little mania'. But I had already guessed it by then, and assimilated it.

It used to happen mainly on buses when I was accompanying him every Thursday to the Art Institute, or in restaurants, or else in the lounge of an airport, if we were on our way to the Cini Foundation in Venice, or to London or Munich for an exhibition, or to Los Angeles for a conference. In other words, in places where there was nothing much to do except wait, and where people, all the strangers surrounding us, unmoving, left to themselves, put their thoughts to rest, withdrew, unaware of their environment for nobody around them aroused their attentions and enlivened their faces. What is the difference between the eyes of a man who doesn't look at anything because he thinks, and the eyes of a man who doesn't think at all? Neither of them sees what's in front of him. One's mind is empty, the other thinking. How to differentiate them? An imperceptible nuance in the pupil that my uncle taught me to decipher.

Suddenly I would notice that something had changed in his eyes, a hardly perceptible shift. A slight closing of his eyelids, almost immediately accompanied by a slight change in his lips, the beginning of a smile. It took me a while before I detected what had just happened in his mind. Oriental storytellers invented the flying carpet to travel in space. Uncle Charles had made himself a little mental device to travel in time while looking at people, with as much ease as Abdullah or Prince Chen Sang on his carpet of clouds. The woman seated opposite him in the bus, who was looking out at the boutiques on the Boulevard St-Germain, or the young girl who smiled at her companion, or the colourless face of the old man with washed-out pupils, my uncle didn't look at them exactly as they were. Once his eyes were fixed on them, having set in motion his little zoom to go back in time or venture forward into the future, he surreptitiously transported himself twenty years later or thirty years earlier. The hint of a smile which appeared then, more in his eyes than on his lips, was neither the sign of irony—of which he was totally incapable—nor malice, nor really even humour. It was the sign of the incredible, truly magical distance he had just put between himself and everything before his eyes. He could discern with extraordinary precision in that young woman with a full and firm face, round cheeks and beautiful lips, the creasing of her eyelids, the curve of her cheeks, the outline of her mouth, what she would become as a grandmother. That big man who looked over the heads of other passengers, uncle examined his face as a twenty year old. He rubbed away the thick furrows that encircled his cheeks, rebuilt the smooth forehead and furbished it with straight hair. He contemplated the fleshy lips, barely marked with something that didn't yet exist, but was already there, and that, thirty years later, would squeeze them with a kind of violence into the avarice of self. When the situation allowed it, he would whisper to me: "The nose. Look at the nose." And I knew I shouldn't look at that nose, but at another, the same but twenty years earlier, or thirty years later, when the wings would be more deeply marked, when a network of small purple veins would colour them, much less because of a well-fed gluttony than because of greediness, and when the fold between the thick eyebrows would have hardened its root.

"Look, Pierre. When his cheeks puff out, as they do when one is fifty, when they will slightly sag on either side of his chin, the line you can discern near the mouth will have become a deep wrinkle. Then his face will show bitterness. He doesn't know it yet, but it is already there. Sometimes he suffers, he is unhappy, he is dissatisfied and he doesn't know why or what for. In thirty years it will be visible. What I mean is not only that he is suffering, but that he doesn't know why."

Or else:

"Look how she must have been pretty … "

But by saying 'look', he was asking me precisely not to see. I had to go beyond the gaze, and invent, and imagine. In my uncle's smile I could read: "I hope she has been loved properly. Yes, I think so … " And in his smile, I could read the explanation: "If she hadn't been, that would be visible … " One had to follow rules, extrapolate rigorously, decipher on an old woman's face the signs, traces, clues of a happiness fifty years old. I looked at my uncle and his smile, then turned my eyes towards the old woman, affectionately of course. I tried to make out how one could be sure she had been properly loved. And, generally, I managed.

Uncle Charles was never content with the present moment. For him, the present was only a small part of reality. The present, the immediate, was only a starting point from which he reconstructed a broader totality. He was never satisfied with what he used to call 'the first look', by which he meant simply, a look. He had to invent other ways of looking to give depth to what he saw and to unfold what the present moment was made of, what it was the conclusion and the result of, then what it was already in the process of becoming.

"Take your time, Pierre, take your time … Titian took five years to do a portrait. Rembrandt painted himself thirty times, which amounts to the same thing. One needs to dig deeply into a face just as one digs deeply into a question."

I understood his passion for the art of portraiture by watching him contemplate faces in the street and on buses. This man, who liked nothing better than faces frozen in a painting, could see there a thousand times more than in a face, living, moving and changing. "A minor painter paints what he sees," he used to say. "One recognizes a great painter in that, in what he shows, he puts everything there is, and everything else. He paints a young princess and the whole woman is present, even what she doesn't know about herself, even what she hasn't yet lived, even what she perhaps won't live but should have lived because her face said so. Because of a fault in destiny, it's possible it will never happen.

"Do you remember, Pierre, that passage in *Anna Karenina* when Konstantin Levin meets Anna for the first time? He has never seen her, he only knows what people say about her, and even before seeing her, while he is waiting, slightly uneasy in the sitting room, he finds himself face to face with her portrait. He is startled, overwhelmed. Suddenly he hears a voice behind him. He turns around and there she is: alike, different, alive. He doesn't know what to look at any longer. He looks at what is between: between Anna and Anna's portrait. If you read the long chapter carefully where Tolstoy narrates Anna and Vronski's stay in Italy, you will understand that what is 'between' is him, Mikhailov, the painter. You are forced to think about him, there, alive, brush in hand, between Anna and her portrait. Levin knows nothing about him, he doesn't know him, but he is forced to guess at that presence. I don't know what Tolstoy knew about painting, but in this extraordinary passage of that extraordinary novel, he offers us one of the greatest and most profound secrets of the art of painting: to see what is 'between'."

My memory refuses to let me hear the sound of her voice. I move around, I mark time, I turn it over in my head. I can't hear it. Sometimes I feel I'm very close to it, imagine that I need only close my eyes, screw my eyelids even tighter, make a bit more silence inside me: the voice is there lurking, elusive like the smell of mushroom. Another effort and I will hear it. I hear it: but immediately I realise my memory is sending back the words, not the sound. I remember the pleasure I felt listening to her talking. My ears strained to savour the melody of her sentences and I sometimes caught myself being more attentive to the musical tones of her voice than to what she was saying. She made flights towards the shrill as the laugh she gave at the end of her sentences approached. I waited for it. It was as if what she was saying needed to be concluded with a pure melody, as if for her, each word pronounced had, in order to go to the bottom of what she was saying, to fold on itself and slip directly into the inner happiness that lived in her. It exploded like a peal at the end of the sentence, a kind of small bell, a trill which got caught at the last syllable after bringing it to its heights. And then it dropped as swiftly into a more tender, mellower tone which said: 'How happy I am about what I just said to you! Look at me, take me, carry me away, I am yours, I love being loved … '

That night, in the darkness of my room, having given up trying to sleep, in my head I turned over not the sound, but the thought of the sound of Judith's voice. For the first time I caught a glimpse of what a musician's memory must be like. I'd never thought about that before. I envy those people for whom sounds have a substance, a mass, as colours and shapes, movement and lines have for me. I remembered the special pleasure I had listening to Judith's voice when she was speaking a language unknown to me: Ukrainian, the language of her parents and grandparents. That is what I call pure music. The words she pronounced played no part in the charm of what, coming directly from her throat, flowed within me, and so her speaking was entirely like her laugh, wordless. I savoured the sound as one appreciates a sonata. I fell asleep reciting to myself names taken from my memories of novels. I whispered: Natalia Petrovna, Ivan Vassilievitch. I repeated them in the darkness of my night. I chewed them in my mouth, awaiting their flavour: Natalia Petrovna, Ivan Vassilievitch, Boris Godounov, Stepan Arkadievitch Oblonski. And then, her own name, mingled with an old biblical perfume: Judith Vycherova, which she had taught me to pronounce properly: Vycht-chie-rova, and which I savoured in my mouth. I summoned my memory, which I had thought of as unfailing for such a long time, and which betrayed me by abandoning me, alone in the night.

Your memory, uncle … We all admired your memory. You were always surprising us. We were in ecstasy, we listened to you open-mouthed, like the crowd around a conjurer who makes white rabbits pop out of his hat, but with you, it was characters, paintings, dates from the whole of history, the paragraphs of articles written by specialists, the exact sentence, without a word missing, the reference, the note, the classification. For us, you were a kind of flute-playing fakir. We didn't know if we should watch the little ballet his fingers danced on the wooden pipe, or the triangle of the snake's head rising up, flicking its forked tongue and uncoiling its body. Your memory, you must know uncle, made us jealous. It fascinated us as if we were the snake. Eyes fixed upon you, we listened to you unwind the strands, unroll the thread. Can I confess that I, your disciple, I set, with a naivety that was immediately crushed, I won't say traps (a waste of time …) but baits, lures, attempts at hooks. I pretended to pick out a minor detail for the sheer pleasure of seeing you unreel the line, pull the thread so much further than I could have imagined, and discover at its end, hundreds of small fish I didn't expect or, rather, that, from experience, I expected, I was hoping for, confirming your infallibility and making us rejoice in the admiration we had for you! Your memory, uncle! …

My memory … Last night, again, like yesterday, I paced around and around Judith's voice. It forces me to ask questions about my memory which never would have come to mind before. Yesterday I wrote: the memory of my eyes. But was it really that? I was complaining that that little symphony of her voice and her laughter only reached my mind through an abstraction which dried them and only represented the ideas or images and not the sounds. I tried to concentrate, I withdrew into myself, as I often do in order to rack my brain, when I try to find the touch of a brush, the control of a hand, the tremor or trembling of a dry-point etching. I know exactly what a hand thinks. My memory forgets nothing of the movements it uses to sweep a surface. I recognize its manner, its flow, its agility or hesitations, its delays, its levellings or supports. But outside that space, I am lost. And sound leaves no trace in space. However, last night, in the dark, I sensed Judith's voice was closer than ever. I knew I was on the verge of hearing it, even if my memory still denied it. I tried to enclose it in a real place, to encircle it, to find a space for it once more, since it is only there my mind is capable of moving. And the place was our bedroom in Venice. I saw once more the windows, their yellow curtains, the flowered wallpaper, the bedside lamp and its dull light. The words came back first, names of painters: 'Bellini, yes! Antonello da Messina, yes!' In that 'yes', in its vertically rising pitch, I sensed the sound of her voice, but without reaching it yet. I sought a substance that would give it body, which touch of saffron yellow should be applied to discover once more that velvety softness of her throat and her laugh, in which proportion to dilute it in oil for it to spread, diffuse, become even more unctuous, what exact dose of caresses one had to add with the tip of the brush.

So colour gave me back Judith's voice and immediately struck a blow to my heart: the fluid, warm yellow, sliding towards dark ochre and turning in scrolls to the hem of the dress in Tintoretto's Visitation, *at the Scuola di San Rocco. I heard: 'I like that … I like … ', and that word had exactly the tone of that hot, unctuous ochre, softly luminous and oily, exactly that tender involution I looked for every night. I didn't hear her voice at first, but the reverberation full of colours of the big lower gallery of the Scuola, as if a screen were still needed; then, inside that echo, Judith's voice with these words: 'Wait a minute … ', that I recognised from the way she used to link words as nobody does any more, and that I imagined came from her mother Sarah, or her grandfather speaking his cautious and polished French with a Ukrainian accent.*

That blow to the heart, that rending, I first thought they had no other cause than the sound rediscovered, that I'd just heard at last. That exquisite kindness of Nature which had provided Judith with what is called a fault of the tongue, which made her soften, mollify, tender in her teeth the trait of pronunciation she inherited from her mother and grandfather: 'Wait a minute … ' The exact transposition on her lips of the voluptuous sweetness of her soul. 'Wait a minute…', 'I want a … '

I repeated two or three times: 'I want a … ', and then, at once, my mind went blank.

All those detours of thought, that labyrinth followed step by step amid the sounds, those detours through colours and the yellow of Elizabeth's dress, that blind quest, those meanders and tricks of memory, were they there only to delay those words lurking in the silence deep within me, for God knows how long, and which I could allow to come back close enough to me for me to say them: 'I want a child … , I want a child with you … '

I cannot bear that memory.

Uncle Charles had torn out the next page. I stared at the small toothed fringe along the fold of the notebook. I stroked it with the tip of my finger. What had you written on this page, uncle? What had you written that I shouldn't read? Why did you tear it out? What additional mistrust or precaution, in case, one day, in fifty years time, someone happened to open that notebook? Or, rather, was it something you wouldn't let yourself think about? Something you couldn't bear the memory of, something you couldn't bear even to have shaped on paper?

How could I? How could I have lived for such a long time so close to someone, been present every day at his side, followed his thought, guessed it, and known nothing about who he really was? Is it I who's the idiot, so deprived of insight, so incapable of sensing what went on in the mind and heart of he with whom I spoke every day? Why did I never ask anything about your inner life, your past, your present, about what was not your work and your research? Everything appeared so simple and so smooth. Your eyes lovingly fixed (that I knew, I could see, I shared) on Elizabeth's blazing yellow dress, as she leaned tenderly towards the Virgin in Tintoretto's sweet *Visitation*. You made me love it. I still love it among all the paintings by that painter I love. How did I not even sense your emotion could come from something else, could hold your heart for an unforeseeable reason? That the trembling of your soul could be linked to an emotion that was not only painted, but which could be yours, and linked to that suffering … How can one be so blind? But, uncle, you never stopped muddying the tracks. You talked to me about beauty and art. I can still see your finger following Tintoretto's brush in this big curve of a golden yellow scroll. You turned to me, smiling: "See that, Pierre?" How could I possibly understand? And now, you have torn out the page. To stop me reading it? Or is it because you yourself didn't want that memory? The following page started in the middle of a sentence.

… the slope which will lead to old age and death. For the last time, one is told one is a man. That he is a man, it's true, the proof is given.

I want a child with you. And that it's the last time: that is not said, but he knows it. And that delicious and irresistible temptation is offered to him by what he holds dearest, in tenderness and from her mouth. The illusion that something can be started all over again, that everything that was imperfect in his life, everything that failed, everything he couldn't do, he will be able to correct. As if one insisted that time could be not entirely irreversible. And he has to say No. Not only say No, but impose on a beautiful and fertile young woman the thought that her love must stop within her and remain sterile. How could I? How could I?

How could I have forgotten? Since finding Judith's voice once more, waves of memories are returning. When I was a child, the man we called the hammerer placed and replaced metal sheets across the irrigation channels. He flooded some fields, drained others, and I admired that master of water. A flood like those he caused by raising his metal sheets has been released and inundates me. How could I have forgotten?

We are at the far end of the Jardin du Luxembourg, in front of the Art Institute. We had taken care to mark the date of our anniversary: one year since I first saw you. It was March. We had lunch in the same restaurant, but contrary to the previous year, it was raining. I remember you in your grey raincoat, or was it black, I can't remember, glistening with rain as night fell. We didn't hold hands. I was afraid to look ridiculous, a man with grey hair holding hands with a young woman. We talked about ourselves. We were silent. After a pause, I said: 'Twelve months.' I repeated: 'Twelve months.' I placed in that number, that every civilization in the world has glorified with symbols and sanctity, all the tenderness I was capable of, and a kind of pride. I allowed the scenes to run before my eyes. You and me in our first restaurant. You and me in the roof-top of the museum. Not yet in Venice, we were preparing to go there. I repeated: 'Twelve months.' And in the silence that followed, with perhaps the same tenderness, and no sadness yet, for you don't know yet, you placed your hand on my arm and said: 'We could already have a three month old baby ... ' You were thinking about it already.

When one loves, one enters eternity. I didn't know that, hard old man as I had been till then. I thought it was only in the paintings of the great masters that lovers could look at each other for eternity, without the night ever falling, without old age ever creeping in, without tiredness, fatigue or boredom ever appearing. I had just discovered that the stillness of eternal lovers (the Jewish fiancée, Oh Judith, as Rembrandt bequeathed her to us for ever) could give way to looks, fleeting smiles, and momentary glances. As soon as I discovered that, I saw the other side. The day I refused to have a child with you, because I wanted to protect you, because I didn't want you tied to a man already on the downward slope, I knew that our love would end. Some time would elapse. We would still love each other. The taste we had for each other would give us some respite, as would our love for paintings and beauty. But one day, it would end. I understood that our love was mortal, and to believe that is to begin to love no longer.

I have been chained to my armchair for two days now, a blanket over my legs. The attack came exactly when I expected it: a rendezvous, in a way. It is three days since I found Judith's photograph. Something has gone hollow within me that I don't understand, and that frightens me.

For years now, when I stand, walk, bend down, raise my arms, it has hurt, and for years I've been awaiting and dreading those severe winter attacks, during which I can do nothing with my body. That no longer surprises me. I've become accustomed to it. I get by as best I can. I have made arrangements. In winter I spend my days in this armchair, as it doesn't prevent me thinking or working. It doesn't prevent me from being, nor even sometimes taking pleasure in being, when something good or useful comes into my mind. I am less to be pitied than my farmer neighbour's old dog. He is no less impotent than me, but he doesn't know what to do with himself. He can no longer run, sniff here and there all those invisible things that delight a dog's nose. He cannot bark for the sheer pleasure of letting the postman know that he is at home and that he has to ask permission before coming closer. Me, in my armchair, where I sat heavily, until yesterday I still had the advantage over him of being the man of my work, of my knowledge. I could still sniff a little enigma and endeavour to resolve it. I could still hunt in the jumbled footnotes of my erudite colleagues. I could still be myself with a few little things to find out and, who knows, perhaps still, some unsuspected grand little idea to excavate, plough, dig into. Until the day before yesterday. For years this forced immobility, when the winter attack arrives, has distressed me. Some days, my pains give rise to fits of anger and revolt. No one has the right to do this to me, I still have work to do, I have not finished. But other days, I've thought they were useful and that by forcing me to think of nothing else but what was worthwhile, by compelling me to abandon subordinate and minor occupations, they helped me. The pain freed me from the need to distract myself. It kept away unwelcome visitors. Nobody could demand that I do what I didn't want to do. I could only look out at my garden from one single viewpoint, through one window, but it had become a painting, still and yet changing, as if all of Claude Monet's gardens could follow in succession before my eyes: light playing on one side, evening on the other. The shadow of a brown prunus branch contrasted with the yellow autumn foliage of the birch behind it. The blue morning mist faded away, returning, gilded over, in the evening. When one has become accustomed to the idea that a walk is forbidden, it is rather beautiful to discover that things change without moving. Only my hand becoming stiff on the white page tormented me sometimes, letting me glimpse the moment when I would no longer be able to write. Immobile, reclusive, I was however still myself.

My poor uncle. I can see him in the winter days when he was in pain. Not diminished, not embittered, he always wore the same smile, his eyes attentive over his glasses, his mind painstakingly constructing the polite sentences with which he addressed Mariette, and me ("Pierre, would you be kind enough to shed light on a detail that is bothering me … "). Never harsh nor bad-tempered, but secretly humiliated. Without saying so, of course. Without complaining, without even asking for a helping hand to stand up or climb the stairs ("So sorry, Pierre ... This old carcass ... "). Yes, humiliated, but for that old man of the past, what one meant by humiliation at a time when society had erected codes of honour: To be placed in a situation where his dignity was scoffed at, and without any means to regain it. Poor uncle. I had understood that it was better not to pity him, not to even notice his weakness. One day I saw him looking at his hand holding that silver propelling pencil he always carried, as he always had his white scarf, and I read, I'm certain I read in his eyes, in the space of a moment: "And when my hand is no longer able to write ... "

Me, here, in this bed, barely capable of stretching my arm to switch my light on or off, taking up a book, or plumping my pillow, me, here. Was it me who ran through the alleyways of Venice holding hands with a young woman? Was it me who, having rediscovered an unthought-of-strength, climbed at the double and the rhythm of her youth, the steps of the countless and exhausting hump-backed bridges which cross the canals of that flat city where one never stops climbing stairs? He who was witness to the images that loom within me these two days, is it still me? Me looking at Judith from the top of a bridge and delaying the moment when our eyes will meet, was it me and is it me who feels now the same fear to see before me the image of Judith? How could I have forgotten? How could I have lived so many years, having forgotten her? It is not from being crippled and frozen that I suffer; it is not being sure of recognising myself in this emotion that rises in me today. The old man who is moved by what moved the younger man, is it or is it not the same man? Me, am I me?

Why make the effort to write all this, exhausting my poor hand a little more? Taken aback, I've opened this notebook in the early hours, with the sole aim of recording things that concern only myself. I carry on writing for no good reason, with difficulty and with a pain which—I no longer know—may come from my hand or maybe my hand, translating into words the pain I feel, transcribes the pain itself. My hand, me. What does that mean?

Nobody will read these lines. Nobody should ever read them. Why write them then? Throughout my working life, I have felt compelled to make notes. But when I forced my hand to blacken the pages, it was to write down useful things, that I was the only one to know, and facts, and discoveries I had to pass on. Why did I start writing to myself of things I don't understand?

Pardon me, Uncle Charles. You are telling me (but you don't know it is me you are telling) I shouldn't read you. I've read you already. Can I pretend I haven't?

I didn't sleep the other night, for the forgotten images slowly returned, or is it that I thought I'd forgotten them, as if for years I had only lived on the surface of myself. Each thought, each memory, as they came back (but where were they coming back from?), helping and supporting each other, had undertaken to burrow a cavern within me, a tunnel, an oubliette (what a word!), or perhaps a kind of ants-nest with countless galleries, a subterranean labyrinth of minute passages teeming with minute bustling thoughts, crossing paths, tapping each other with their antennae, acknowledging each other, and proceeding on their way in the dark. At one point in the night I suddenly understood what the Ancients in their mythology called the Labyrinth. One thinks it's an underground passageway somewhere in the world, in Crete, or Sicily or somewhere else, in the world of things, forms and distances, whereas this Labyrinth is nothing but the shapeless subterranean world that everybody carries within them and down where they fear to venture for it is dark in there and they are frightened, terribly frightened that right at the bottom there will really be a Minotaur. And everybody gropes in the dark and shouts: 'Ariadne, my sister, your thread, where is your thread?'

Here I am having mythological nightmares ...

I almost saw the sunrise. Why do nights of insomnia end when dawn appears, and why does one drop into that thick, massive, absolute sleep that leaves no room for dreams, after a night spent vainly seeking it? A grey line had already appeared between the curtains that Mariette had drawn yesterday evening, first completely, then halfway when asked her to. Each day ends with that small battle. She pulls, draws, crosses the material so that nothing, not one beam of moonlight, not one star can reach me, not one noise. And each evening: 'Draw them back a little, please, Mariette.' 'But, monsieur Charles, you'll get cold.' 'Don't worry, I'm well covered.' Unhappy, she draws them back reluctantly by two centimetres. 'If you cough tomorrow, don't ask me why.' People from the countryside fear the night. They have centuries-old fears in their heads, of wolves, bandits, witches and the cold. Thus I am left with one line of moonlight across the bedroom, which turns with the hours like the hands of a clock, and that I confuse with dawn. But today it really was dawn. My night was almost entirely spent floating between kinds of drowsiness, tossing and turning my poor body in my bed, and in my head, one single thought. If the nights are more painful than the days, it is because my stretched limbs are even more vulnerable than when I sit in my armchair. Each position in which I settle seems for a short while a wonderful respite. I don't suffer any longer … and almost immediately it generates another pain, in another part of my back, or my shoulder, or my leg, which seems worse than the one before. I need to turn again, which takes a long time, with the illusion that lying in another position I will stop suffering, or will suffer less, or differently.

But last night, the same thing happened in my head. That one thought obsessed me and I couldn't stop turning it round and one, trying it one way, then another. When I made the effort to push it away, it came back at an angle, barely disguised. It is me, me, who left Judith. It is me who left. I went down the steps, suitcase in hand. I left. It is me who decided never to see her again, ever. So that never would she have the opportunity to say to me: 'I want a child.' I left her so as not to have to fight this battle against myself and against her and to answer: 'No, I don't want, we cannot, it's not possible.' I sat up, stretched out my arm, groaning, to turn on the light by my bed. I looked at my hand and my arm and told

43

myself: here is the hand, here is the arm of that child's father, Judith's child, when he would be twenty. Can one be a father when one doesn't have the strength to be a man any longer? When I said No, *with self-loathing, disgust, shame.*

I don't believe you, uncle. That you suffered, that your suffering body dragged your mind into that night sorrow, I can believe that, I grieve with you. How could I have perceived nothing at all? You concealed the suffering of your soul behind that of your limbs. But disgust, shame and loathing, no, I don't believe you. Uncle, I don't believe you.

... when I said No *while looking at Judith in tears, when I willingly broke the sprit of our love, 'no, we cannot, we ought not to have a child because of my age,' when I broke off her joy and drew away from her with a mighty self-control, what was I doing? Yes I took that for heroism, I anticipated her tears, I was ashamed of myself and pitied her. But did I do it for all the good reasons I repeated to myself, or was it through cowardice? Answer, bed-ridden cripple. A child, at your age? Look at your hand. Turn over. Stretch your back. How old would she be when you're groaning in your bed each time you turn over? Member of the Institute. Emeritus Professor of American universities,* honoris causa. *Laugh, my colleagues. A woman, young, attractive, sweet. Yes: a child. Which is shameful: to be ridiculed in a conference or by Judith's tears? Answer. When a woman asks you to fertilise love, what does one answer? When she says to you (she said it to me, she plunged that dagger into my chest, I remember her words exactly), when she says that she wants love to give birth to life, does one say* No *without being a coward? She thought that, Your Honour. She told me that: 'The proof of love must be born from love.' And me, I said* No. *'Love must produce the proof of love, provide the public proof (and she said: public) of love, the child it bears.' Does one say* No *if one is not a coward, or a hypocrite? Answer, you old fossil.*

I awoke with a sentence in my mind that I'd written two days before, a proof that every minute my sleep must have pondered it: 'I understood

*that our love was mortal, and to believe that is to begin to love no longer.'
Every night, do I then recite to myself what I wrote during the day?*

*To love no longer. Did I live so many years without loving any longer?
How could I live so many years without thinking, almost without
thinking, almost without ever thinking about Judith? Had I buried
that memory so deep in order to be sure it could no longer come to
the surface? As one buries remorse? Through fear? Through shame?
Through willingness to conceal from myself how pitiful was the life I
led, an old bachelor without affection, without aim, without … Did I
just want to avoid asking myself: did you fail your life? Did I immerse
a few weeks of my life in oblivion because I sensed that by remembering
my walking away I would have to admit that it marked the beginning
of a failed life? What have I done with my life?*

*Not a day, not an hour had we ceased being occupied by painting.
Occupied as one says of a country, or captured like prisoners chained
in a jail. But instead of chains, what held us were the innumerable
metamorphoses of happiness, transfigured from one moment to the
next by our appetite for beauty which never stopped inventing new
ways to regale itself. It was not enough to spend our afternoons at the
Accademia, at the Scuola di San Rocco, to rush again and again to the
churches to see the Carpaccio in San Giorgio dei Schiavoni, the Tiepolo
in Santa Maria dei Gesuati, the Bellini in San Zaccaria, to haunt
palaces hoping to unearth an unknown painting. Our desires were rarer,
more secretive. We would cross the whole of Venice in our impatience
to gaze on a painting by the young Tintoretto, in San Marcuola. We
would dash to the Madonna dell'Orto to see again an* Annunciation
*by Palma il Giovane. It was a jubilation, an exultation, a rapture.
But churches, museums and palaces were not sufficient. We took in
everything: a ray of sun on a section of a façade and its reflection in
the canal, the glimpsed profile of a Venetian woman with curly hair,
a sheen of mist on San Giorgio Maggiore. When we walked in the
narrow and sinuous alleyways, when we passed along the canals in
remote districts, it was as if we were on the lookout, like hunters in a*

forest or mushroom-pickers. We hardly spoke, entirely absorbed in this kind of hunt. In Venice, the unpredictable can spring out at any turn, like a fox at a bend in a forest track or a partridge above a furrow. Even what one knows, what one expects, can take one by surprise. One stops, taken aback, like on the very first day, happy, even happier, because of that small extra joy of meeting again. At the corner of an alleyway, she would come to a standstill, stretch out her arm, trace a rectangle in the air in which she enclosed section of wall, a Gothic window, a landing-stage, and turn her head towards me: 'Tironi … ', or 'Bellotto'. Or she would mark out with her hand a fragment of sky of a delicate fleecy blue with incredible white and pink clouds: 'Tiepolo!' Or even nothing, only her smile, since she knew that my expertise on this virtual painting would reach the same conclusion.

I see her. I see her perfectly. She pauses suddenly near a small bridge spanning a narrow canal. She touches my arm and with her hand shows me a still black dog chewing on something behind the stone railing, only its rear and trumpet-like tail visible. 'Look … ' For a moment I trawl my memories. A stupid shame rises from my chest to my head. I think I'm really at a loss. My memory comes back just in time and I have to unknot my nerves before I can answer. 'What's missing is a blind beggar with his back to the railing … ' She laughs. She puts her arm around my neck. 'A very good answer, Professor. A barrel is also missing from it.' 'And it's not the Rialto.' Pedantic, still slightly anxious at the thought I was going to have to keep quiet, gone dry as if before an oral examination, with my pupil as examiner, I almost add: 'Michele Marieschi.' I refrain just in time. And then, the pedant becomes more subtle, or rather the emotion of having thought I would fail, demands revenge for my vanity. I say: 'Leningrad Museum … ' She laughs again and kisses me.

Excuse me, Professor. Leningrad is no longer, St Petersburg is what we call it now. You are out-dated, I think … Immediately I start. A date! Finally a possible dating! Here is the first indication Uncle Charles has given me of the era he describes in this notebook. My dear uncle, I, too, am on the trail. I am your disciple. You have taught me that everything must be dated and that is why, while reading you, I can't stop looking for a reference, a marker, something to cross-check in your pages. And this time, I have it. Thank you, uncle, for the method. In what year did Leningrad become St Petersburg? 1990? 1991? Easy to check … I … Well, no. It's worth nothing and doesn't teach me anything. I too went to the Accademia, to San Giorgio dei Schiavoni. We went together. You were still walking, painfully, slowly, already with that severe air that infirmity gradually gave to your features. Years must have passed between what you relate and the strolls we took, me holding your arm to help you walk, and you with your walking stick in your left hand. When Leningrad was called St Petersburg again, you were already crippled with pain in your armchair. Our last journey dated back five years at least and already you weren't walking easily. We used to take the vaporetto at San Giorgio Maggiore, change at San Marco and then we only had to take a few steps, which were hard for you, to enter the Accademia. How old do I need to imagine you, Uncle Charles, kissing a young woman in the streets of Venice?

I knew she had never been to Leningrad and could only have seen that painting in a book. I knew which one. We remained entwined for some time. I opened my eyes again, I looked over her shoulder at that black half-dog and wondered: what a coincidence? Is it that painting by Michele Marieschi, a sub-Canaletto of average quality, skilful but rather charmless, lost in the collections of the Hermitage? Is it the beauty of the young woman I'm holding in my arms? Is it the complicity between us through the intermediary of colours spread on a canvas? What is the cause of this happiness? Is there a cause, what one calls a cause?

The truth is that during those few days spent together in Venice, she had instilled in me the passion for painting.

Can I really write down that sentence without laughing?

What about me, uncle, can I read it without smiling? Because painting was you … I know, I learnt it from you … I know nothing I haven't learnt from you. Was there ever one moment in your whole life when you didn't have the passion for painting?

Except if … But you are mixing everything up. Is it because a young woman whom I have to imagine attractive, for you say so, accompanies you to Venice, that suddenly Venice is transfigured ? Me too, uncle, me too, I went seven times with you to Venice. I took you everywhere. I was at the Accademia. I was in San Rocco. What were you thinking about when you stopped in front of Bellini's *Virgin*, and when, pointing to the Magdalene, hands clasped on her right, with her soft eyes and her lost gaze, you told me: "She is the most moving woman I have ever seen." When I helped you climb the wooden steps of the bridge leading to the Accademia, uncle, tell me, whom were you thinking of ? And me, at your side, who was I? I am humiliated, uncle. Humiliated.

I: this man who, for fifty years, hasn't cared about anything else. I who never had any other preoccupation than to know more and more paintings, more drawings and sketches, to compare them, analyse them, identify them, date them and even love them, I the expert. Here I am, having just written this sentence where I say that for just a month of my life I had a passion for painting. Am I mad? These memories lead me astray. Can I confuse love, yes, the feeling of being madly in love, being wildly in love, deranged love, with a woman, for a single month, with what has been my entire life for fifty years? How could I write that?

Yesterday evening, I stopped writing.

I sat quietly, not doing anything, not even trying to pick up a book, until Mariette came to bring me my dinner and found me in the semidarkness of nightfall. She thought me ill and began to worry. She helped me to bed and I sent her away somewhat brusquely. I had to ring to make her return so I could apologise. By doing that I think I made my case worse, for now she thinks I am suffering from the beginnings of dementia. That would have been rather amusing if I'd had the heart to laugh. She was staring at me apprehensively. 'Mariette, could you please bring me a book that is on that shelf, on the far right, just at the level of your hand. It is called Albertine Gone. *You can't possibly miss it.' Yes, it is what I was thinking about, while night fell in my work-room. Proust in Venice. Me in Venice. Proust is in love and he leaves his mother, his affectionate mother, whom he couldn't bear, in Combray, when she did not come up to say good night to him in bed, he cruelly abandons her, leaving alone for the station, because he is in love. I wanted to know if, for him, leaving Venice was more painful than leaving a woman, or if Venice and the woman were one, or if it is Venice which generates that kind of wild, mad, confused love. Mariette looked along the shelves of my library. I could hear her grumbling, saying she couldn't find that book, and Sir had made a mistake. 'But, Mariette, it is there, it is. I am certain it's there. The author's name is Marcel Proust. Look again.* Albertine Gone … ' *'But monsieur Charles, I'm telling you it's not here.' We almost had an argument. Her voice was full of anger. 'Proust, Proust, of course I can see him. But it's called* Remembrance of Things Past. *Time's passing by for me too here, you know … ' 'That's it, Mariette. Bring it to me.' 'But you asked me for* Albertine *and now you want things past, how can I know what you want?' Yes, I would have laughed if I'd had the heart to laugh. Mariette reminds me of Françoise, the old servant of the aunt in Combray, whom we meet again, become tyrannical now, in* Albertine. *But it is not that. It is the night's slow journey through my curtains that has strangely placed me in a Proustian state of isolation, sadness, and return to what is no more, to what was perhaps never there. Are the memories we have something true, real, present, or are they a construction out of something which isn't any longer but which was, or a construction out of nothing? Is the search for things past the*

remembrance of something, or a perpetual invention? Who was Judith?
Was it true, could I write that, after being taken up with painting
all my life, without the least distraction, I have had the passion for
painting for one month? Yesterday I was tempted to burn this notebook.
I didn't do it. I still don't know why I write these notes, but since I
haven't destroyed what I wrote yesterday, I have to state, yes, state,
claim, although no-one will ever read these lines, state therefore, claim
to myself that I have worked for fifty years on painting but have only
had the passion for painting for one month. Because of her, by her,
through her.

And since last night, I know why.

One evening, one night, we invented a game. I never, at any time in
my life, knew how to play. At twenty I learnt to play bridge, out of
courtesy to my friends.

That is true. One day in the Louvre, in front of *The
Cardsharp* by La Tour, my uncle confessed his ignorance with
a burst of laughter.

"I can see, Pierre, that what he is hiding in his belt while
looking elsewhere is an ace of diamonds. I can see too that
the young man he is going to trick holds several diamonds
in his hand. What I could never succeed in understanding is
why an ace, which is actually a 'one', is worth more than a
'two'. It's illogical. And then why La Tour, who painted the
same painting twice, had him hiding an Ace of Diamonds in
the Louvre, and an Ace of Clubs in the Kimbell Museum.
That's correct, isn't it Pierre? I'm not mistaken?"

I joined in his game. One always had to sniff out the
humour in my uncle's words.

"But, Uncle Charles, it's so that the museum curators can
tell which is which."

He glanced at me mischievously and concluded:

"You are perfectly right. That man thought of everything.
It doesn't surprise me, coming from him. Oh, if all painters

could think for one moment about the problems faced by curators ... Still it's not difficult to sign one's work, to write at the bottom of the painting: me, Rembrandt, *pinxit*, this portrait is a self-portrait. His price will be multiplied by a thousand, even if it's mediocre!"

"Uncle Charles, you forget the fun of the detective story... You would like every murderer to write their name in toothpaste on the bathroom mirror."

"Don't mix everything up. You are going to make me say that a self-portrait by Rembrandt is a murder. But really, you are right. Our profession is partly that of a detective, with the difference that we don't work on horrors, but on beauty."

And, as always, my flash of wit generated a serious reflection for my uncle only considered things, life, the world from the serious side.

"Do you know, Pierre, the object on which men choose to act is as important as their action itself ? So much intelligence for such absurdities ... It diminishes the intelligence."

And with that, he completed the loop. What annoyed him about card games was their uselessness. He told me that his father had tried to teach him chess. All those gratuitous, factitious, futile rules annoyed and irritated him.

"I understand a king being worth more than a knave. That makes sense. But why is a one worth more than a two? And why does a castle move like this and a knight like that? It's arbitrary. Why should I apply my mind to reason on such arbitrariness?"

He added under his breath: "It's like mathematics," looking at me sideways to check if I was walking into his little provocation, then insisted: "I do not say that mathematics doesn't transcribe an aspect of reality, but it is that aspect which holds no interest ... " And to conclude: "I couldn't remember the rules. I was worse than a bad player, I was an absent player … "

It was not a game like those, the one she had invented that night in our bed in Venice. It was resolutely childish, infantile compared to bridge or chess. Curiously, it placed me back in my position as professor, opposite her as a schoolgirl. But it reversed the roles, or rather, turned them upside down, as the jester parodies the court. My role consisted in enumerating the names of painters, all the painters I could think of, right down to the rarest and least known. And that is when the game became fun and when, for more laughter, my function as an examiner split in two. I would cite their names and the game consisted of her shouting out her love for this one, her disdain for another, and transforming into shrieks of delight the evocation of their names. It was totally childish, but as children do, I wanted to continue this game indefinitely. I was doing my best to provoke all the possible manifestations of enthusiasm. I carried on pronouncing the painters' names for the sheer pleasure of seeing on her face and in the tone of her voice, all the beauty of her joy appearing and blooming. I said: 'Carpaccio!' She screamed: 'Yes!' 'Masaccio!' 'Yes, yes!' 'Delacroix!' 'Yes!' 'Fragonard!' 'Oh yes!' 'Claude Monet!' 'Nope!' and doubled her giggles to underline the provocation of that sacrilegious 'Nope'. 'Antonello da Messina!' 'Yes, yes!' And in that range of 'yes', in the greater or lesser elevation of her voice, in the brightening of her face with laughter, in the pure gaiety of her eyes, I discovered, I the scholar, the expert, the professor, the love of beauty. 'Bellini!' 'Yes, yes, yes!' Setting a trap, I started laughing: 'Giovanni, or Gentile?' 'Giovanni!' 'Or Jacopo?' 'Giovanni!' I knew she was not going to confuse Bellini the father with his two painter sons. But I felt just then a great affection for her, a tenderness made of everything that came together in that moment. Her beauty, the beauty of her breasts full like those of a Venetian who could have been painted by Giorgione or Titian. My taste for everything to do with art, that she transformed in me by stripping it of what thirty years of research and study had done to it, transforming it into jubilation, as if she herself had changed into a painting, metamorphosed into a Bellini angel or a Giorgione Venus, herself haloed with gold on the pillow, or the waves of her hair transformed into Danaë's gold. This is what I found that night, at about two or three in the morning, and which made me understand what I had written yesterday. It is in remembering the details of our game that I was able to grasp it. For I remembered that, as I knew in advance which painters she was going to greet with shrieks of joy, I too entered the painting along with the game, I preceded her in her enthusiasm, in what yesterday I called passion. I took pleasure in her happiness even before she shrieked, so that the desire which slowly rose in us as the game went on—I couldn't tell if it was born out of the evocation of beauty, or of the enumeration of all the miracles of beauty, or if this litany ('Jacobello del Fiore!' 'Yes!' 'Andrea Schiavone!' 'Yes!') were weaving a kind of spell, or if it was born of that progressive communion in happiness, or if the excitement, the laughter,

The notebook stopped there, on a comma, at the evocation of desire. Discreet Uncle Charles who, even in that secret notebook that nobody (he had written that himself), nobody should ever read, even there, couldn't translate into words feelings that were too intimate and too strong.

Or else too painful?

PART TWO

NOTHING PREPARED ME for my meeting with Judith, several years later, in a small annexe of the University of Rome, during a conference on Art History. It even seemed as if everything had been arranged to heighten my surprise. Even the name shown on the programme had been cleverly tweaked. What link could I have made between the young woman in fits of laughter in my uncle's bed and what was announced in the austere programme of this scholarly conference?

'University of Rome, 10.30 a.m. Judith Desgranges of the University of Paris-Sorbonne: Treatise on perspective in Brunelleschi.'

Even her name was disguised …

I was prepared to be bored. It was not for Brunelleschi that I had come to this conference and that I had spent a sleepless night in a couchette of the Paris-Rome train, but for a very particular subject: some drawings by Sebastiano del Piombo and Domenico Campagnola that had just been discovered in one of those Italian villas where hidden treasures emerge as the old Italian families rummage in their attics in order to survive a bit longer. So I was there that morning more out of politeness than curiosity, waiting for the lecture which interested me and for, I confess, the lunch too (I love Italian food) during which I could chat with some colleagues who were friends. Waiting, I sat like a schoolboy on the hard benches of that sad, grey, badly lit amphitheatre, amongst specialists from Princeton, Harvard, Oxford and Göttingen, all of them sat like schoolboys too. Like them I was dozing, after that long night without sleep. I barely paid attention to the woman who had just appeared on the official platform, slightly plump, her blond hair already greying and cut short, and who was introduced with a very Roman emphasis by the President of the session. "Mrs Judith Desgranges, whose important work on the Art of the Quattrocento and areas of expertise are not unknown to us, etc … " Today, when I think again about that moment and the emotion rises in me afresh, I sense once more, in its incredible progression, the succession of augurs, warning signs, then the confusion, a kind of useless unsteadiness, then panic. I am amazed I didn't guess there and then who that mature plump woman was, learned and focused, to whom I listened while, little by little, my uncle's sentences came back to me in counterpoint to what I was hearing.

The first alert, the first as yet indecipherable thrill came before she even opened her mouth, when the profusion of rhetorical praises from the President of the session made her burst out laughing. "Mrs Judith Desgranges has too much finesse for the vanishing point of the perspective according to Brunelleschi to … " She started laughing, with a laughter as uninhibited as the President's speech was inordinately formal. A cascade of shrill notes, splashing down to raucous, fleshy, carnal depths. I lifted my eyes and looked at her. But still I didn't recognise her.

I was feeling too drowsy after my bad night. I was slowly drifting and, only gradually, through the haze of my semi-torpor, the voice of Judith (Judith!) conveyed the second signal, which, initially, I understood no better than the first. The soft and beautiful Italian name of Brunelleschi, constantly brought forth by the subject she was handling, took on a peculiar suavity in her mouth. She pronounced it with the correct accent, rendering all its gracefulness, with a very delicate *Bru* in which the *r* was barely rolled and slightly softened in an *ou*. She made the *s* velvety, and in my half-sleep, I listened to this soft and silky syllable which recurred

"He was a man of infinite learning. I had the opportunity to work with him a few times."

She was still smiling.

"Me too."

I didn't dare look her straight in the eye. Intimidated, confused, as if I'd been caught red-handed. Why red-handed? Must I feel ashamed to know certain things that the woman talking to me doesn't know I know? How am I supposed to look at that woman, when … Uncle, what am I to do? If you loved Judith, what am I to do?

Judith talked to my neighbour:

"I did my thesis thanks to him. I owe him everything … "

She owes him everything, she said … And he, with comic emphasis:

"I know it. You did remarkable work with him. I admire you. I even greatly appreciate that you were able to keep some distance from his method. Didn't you sometimes feel … how shall I say it, tired, if not discouraged by that rigour … "

—he sang the word 'rigour'—

" … and also by, yes, a certain narrowness of conception, if I can dare to say that? Of conception, and, above all, of method … "

What was he trying to say? This time, I glanced at Judith's face. She was looking straight in the eyes of her questioner. Nothing could be read in her eyes. She was still smiling. I stepped in, seeking a way of rectifying this blunder.

"But don't you find that his kindness … "

I had spoken too fast. I stopped short, hesitating, as if I was the blunderer. He swept forward into the gap.

"Yes, his kindness, as you say. He was a 'kind' man." He looked at me before insisting:

"Let's call it his civility. His refined courtesy. Shall I say, he was a man from another era."

I was staring at Judith. A mechanism repeated within me— she doesn't know I know, she doesn't know I know. Our eyes met. I wondered if she still remembered my uncle's words. The bore talked on:

"You understand, for me, art is something else. I'm always surprised that, nowadays, one can still remain an epigone of that purely historicising interpretation of artistic phenomena. One ends up ... yes ... As if one could forget that perspective, since it is about that, dear lady, that you entertained us so brilliantly ... "

And he talked to Judith! It was to Judith that he talked! To Judith!

" ... is given to us, not only as, how can I say, as an interdependent form of a kind of ... a kind of epistemological constellation, you see what I mean? But Charles Millau (God forbid me from saying anything ill about him, or to belittle his erudition), Charles Millau was from another epoch, another school ... "

I didn't take my eyes off Judith now. Her round face, her neck, her motionless half-smile. Our eyes met again and I knew that thanks to that idiot we had become allies. But what was she smiling for?

"But I would like, dear lady, to turn the metaphor around. To strip it. Yes, to strip it of all totalizing connotation. To consider it no more as a kind of ... of paradigmatic apparatus, absolutely, eminently paradoxical ... "

He was savouring his own words. He was tasting them as he pronounced them. He smiled. He looked at Judith and checked her eyes for the swarm of butterflies with which she was about to tell him of the love she felt for 'epistemological constellation' and for 'paradigmatic apparatus'. He gazed at her smile and smiled too, listening to himself resume:

" … and which consequently obeys, beyond any reference to reality (as you so rightly told us), obeys a purely, exclusively symbolic determination … But, pardon me, to confine oneself to a system so exclusively, so tragically historicist, when the perceptive paradigm is so obviously compelled to determinations of a purely structural order which … "

He was singing too on the 'purely structural' but I didn't listen any more. As he was talking, my impatience increased to hear her, to listen to her voice, to finally recognise her. But, while (what was his name?) Pellerin proceeded with his dissertation, spicing it with little treacheries towards the man of whom he knew perfectly well, even if it was the first time he was meeting us, we were both the offspring, she continued to keep her silence. I looked at her lips. I awaited her words. I looked into the shape of her mouth, into the outline of her lips, for the thing that caused the delicate lisp whose memory broke my uncle's heart. Suddenly, like a dart, like a scalding, I heard the voice and Uncle Charles' own words: "Simonetta … On the Chantilly portrait, Pierre, look at the mouth, you can hear her talk … " So, that was it?

Uncle Charles, when you were tenderly drawing with your finger, I saw you, I saw your gaze and your smile, when you were tracing Simonetta's lip in the air with the tip of your finger, those lips as painted by Piero di Cosimo, or Pollaiuolo, Uncle Charles, what were you thinking about? About the beauty of that portrait you taught me to love, or about Judith's lips?

And, at that precise moment, her voice:

"Excuse me, I really have to go … I hope we will have the opportunity to see each other again one of these days … You are staying in Rome till the eighth? Well, see you soon … "

Then, turning to me:

"Mr Voisin, would you care to accompany me?"

We had barely the time to turn our backs and take two steps towards the exit:

"I can't bear that type … "

Two steps further:

"You are Charles Millau's nephew?"

"Yes, it's me. Do you know me?"

"I recognised his white scarf around your neck. Do you always wear it? Will you accompany me to the Piazza Navona? I'm meeting my daughter there."

I followed and immediately the unforeseen meeting began to unwind like a ball of string, a succession of unconnected episodes of which not one seemed to prepare for the next. For the time being, I saw myself transformed, with a kind of keen and covert swiftness, into a naughty pupil who bunks school to follow a girl. I who had made the journey to Rome especially, who had spent a bad night on the sleeper train in order to listen to a scholarly communication on drawings recently recovered and attributed to Sebastiano del Piombo, that painter to whom I had devoted so much attention and work, I had sneaked out of the lecture theatre and was walking in the Via Condotti, looking idly into shop windows alongside Judith … that Judith.

I knew this street by heart. In those shop windows, stripping the Italian women of their chatter, and even of their heads, the dummies provide only a means to analyse and dissect the Roman fashions. It was of course Uncle Charles who, smiling as always, had made me stop one day, and surprised me by pointing to one of those windows. How to imagine he might be interested in fashion? No problem. He started the discussion. "Look, Pierre … Not a single one of those dresses can be seen in Paris. Here, all female stratagems are natural, though seen through a magnifying glass. Magnifying, I mean ... Actually, yes, that's it, even in the proper sense. Curves. One doesn't get rid of Veronese so easily." I repeated Uncle Charles' words to Judith (Judith!). She didn't respond and I didn't understand why at first. Later, when we sat in Piazza Navona, it occurred to me that she already knew my uncle's little speeches.

Meanwhile, it was Judith who, unknowingly, had set me on the trail. We had just passed the Borghese Palace, and stopped for a moment to browse casually through some bundles and books on the stalls of the book dealers when, looking up, she asked:

"Would it bother you if we were to make a small detour before we reach Piazza Navona? Only two hundred metres. I would like to spend a moment in Sant'Agostino."

She didn't need to give me the reasons for this detour. I had guessed.

"I'd like to have a look at the Caravaggio painting ... "

"The Madonna of the Pilgrims?"

"Yes. I haven't had time to see it yet."

That was the first sign of recognition, whose implication I couldn't yet measure completely. She hadn't had time yet ... However hard we tried to blend into the Roman crowd, skirting the strollers in the middle of the road, nothing changed the fact that Uncle Charles was already with us, or between us. I could already almost formulate the sentence Judith was about to pronounce. In my head, I said it before her:

"When I come to Rome ... "

"Usually, when I come to Rome, it's the first visit I make." I laughed. But my laughter was not entirely cheerful, more a nervous laugh.

"A formal visit, in a way?"

An affected laugh, like the word that had come into my

mind. Formal? Formal, the visit Uncle Charles enjoyed making on the first day of each of his stays in Rome? The church he took me to? Formal, the smile I would glimpse on his face as we approached, as we climbed the numerous steps he used to slowly ascend, as if to ready himself for a long-awaited, desired pleasure, the way he used to stop to put his pipe in his pocket before going beyond the porch? Formal? I asked myself: why this bitterness in me? She, untroubled:

"Formal, if you like. I'd rather say I'm going to make my devotions."

Embarrassed. Almost shy.

"Yes, my devotions. That's the right word. It's a painting that moves me. There are paintings one admires and others one is moved by. This one does both at the same time. When I'm in front of it, I almost feel like the old woman one sees in the foreground, kneeling before the Madonna, with her dirty feet. She looks so happy with her old woman smile and her dirty feet. I'm worshipping, exactly like her. If I was a believer, I would say a real prayer."

I wondered whom I was listening to. Her, there, next to me, her hands deep in a pile of old books on a jumbled stall, or my uncle's voice rising inside me as she talked, with the same words, the same images of piety, the same tenderness half-veiled, but not entirely, by some form of modesty. As if both of them were embarrassed to say they were 'moved' and so concealed that crack of emotion under a cloak of affected religious bigotry. I could hear my uncle telling me, as we climbed the steps—how many years ago now? ten? twelve?—in his slightly breathless voice: "Pierre, we should make a visit of devotion to *The Madonna of the Pilgrims.*" The same words. He used to tell me: "No Virgin by any painter, and God knows how many there are in Italy and elsewhere, none is as moving as that one." Uncle Charles used to say "moving". Judith was repeating him. Me too, in fact. Who thought I'd been the only one to make that 'visit of devotion' with him each time we came to Rome.

I looked at Judith's profile as we walked, and bumped into her accidentally. How many times, uncle? How many times, as you climbed the steps with me, as you stopped here to push your pipe in your pocket, how many times did you think of someone other than me? What, whom, were you thinking of when you smiled as you climbed the stairs?

She turned her head towards me:

"It doesn't bother you, this detour?"

"Not at all. I like it too, you know."

I had added "you know" spitefully. She didn't seem to hear it. Of course, how could she have understood?

When one is seated in Piazza Navona, as we were, on the terrace of one of the cafes lined along one of the two sides which monopolise the sun, one feels freed from having to talk. Naturally, it was Uncle Charles who pointed it out one afternoon in April, I think, or perhaps May, at the time of the year when Rome is still fresh and already luminous. "What's the point of forcing oneself, Pierre, don't you think? Elsewhere, in Paris, or even in Vienna, one really has to furnish conversation. Why does one say 'furnish'? Is a conversation comprised of inert objects, furniture, trinkets?" He smiled and lit his pipe again. "A conversation of curios ... After all, perhaps that is what it's all about ... One 'furnishes' when one doesn't have anything to say that is vital and one lays down wooden words between the chatterings, finely carved solid oak words if it's good company, to fill the space that separates us. Silence is like an empty room. What can I do to feel comfortable? Where to sit? Where to rest my eyes? Quick, a trinket to furnish ... Here, looking is a full-time occupation. But not entirely. Pierre, drink up your Martini … " And my uncle and I remained silent for long stretches, under the same green-and-white striped parasols transposing their streaks onto our table, mellowing Judith's features. Behind her, Bernini's immense, baroque fountain heaped with a mass of stacked rocks, populated with lions, neighing horses, bearded giants gesturing to each other with their hands, ("one of them," my uncle used to say with a laugh, "to proclaim the horror inspired in him by the façade of St Agnes, because Bernini hated his rival Borromini,"), and then Neptune and his dolphins, and the red and ochre façades, the fountains, the flowerpots on the balconies, and the people who pass in the street without seeing each other, and the pavement artists who await the tourists to sketch their portraits and imagine themselves Michelangelos. Everything conspires for centuries to saturate our eyes and free us from speaking. That is what uncle used to say.

In truth, Judith and I hadn't uttered another word since we'd sat down. We hadn't needed to discuss which table we would choose to sit at. Without wondering which of those terraces all alike we were going to choose, we had done it without being surprised to have sat at this one rather than another. It was a bit later that I thought we must have our habits. The same ones? … The crowd was not yet as noisy as it would be later in the evening, when the square would be invaded by tourists. The sounds were still distinct, the voices still clear, in counterpoint to the footsteps. Despite the distance, one could even catch the violin of an old man seated far away on the lip of Neptune's basin and playing by himself, as if for himself, without anybody stopping to listen. From time to time, the Englishman seated at our neighbouring table leaned forward to say a few words I couldn't catch, to his pink, curly-haired wife.

At times I let my eyes fall on Judith's face against the background of the cascade and rocks, her beautiful blue eyes, that (how should I say it?) graceful benevolence that emanated from it, accentuated by the fullness brought on by her fifty years, her age underlined by the mass of her short, straight grey hair. How was she at twenty, when she walked in the streets of Rome? Did I ask myself that question? I don't think so. It came to me in the shape of the thought that when he talked about Italian fashion, my uncle no doubt remembered running his eyes over the shop windows of Via Condotti—accompanied by a woman. And I thought, he was still fit when he climbed the steps to the church of Sant'Agostino.

We had just entered Sant'Agostino. The warmth of the Italian baroque had enveloped us like a silky stole round our shoulders. As if my role were written in my personal score, I had established my function, walking a few steps behind, leaning on a pillar, ready to push a coin into the collecting box to keep alight the lamp that was never extinguished. Ten years ago I had made the same gesture, and at the sound of the rattle made by my coin as it dropped, the silhouette of Judith immediately reappeared in the exact place occupied in the past by my uncle, in front of that painting he loved and to which he came to make, and it was his word and not hers, "his devotions".

She made a movement and turned her head towards me.

"I'm going ... "

With a busy, preoccupied air, she explored her handbag, in which her forearm had almost completely disappeared, and foraged anxiously.

"I can't find my purse ... "

"Do you need something?"

The moment a woman finds herself missing something, embarrassed, is the moment a man wakes up.

"No, it's here … "

She turned her head towards Neptune's basin, behind the crowd of passers-by, in the middle of the square:

"I wanted to listen to the old man … "

She was pointing at the violin player still playing there, by himself. We could just hear the sound of his violin, like a minute thread of clarity above the hum of voices and steps.

"Did you notice, nobody stops to listen to him. There is such a mess in my bag … "

She stood and I watched her walk away, her flowered dress blooming in the sun. She circumvented a group of teenagers crowded around a portrait artist, laughing their heads off at the expense of a poor woman sitting there, serious and timid, hunched over her self-esteem that was undoubtedly being mistreated with every stroke of charcoal. I saw Judith pause for a moment, glance over the shoulders of the boys and burst out laughing. I wondered: what does one become, who are we, when we have become the hostage of the person who snatches your face, strips it of what your will, your conscience, your desire imagines it is, and does with it what he wants? Did Anna Karenina like what Mikhailov made of her, and which so surprised Konstantin Levin? Did she see herself in it, did she see her soul?

Judith was standing in the distance, stock still, facing the violin player who carried on playing without lifting his head. I pricked up my ears for the feeble sound of his violin, which was barely audible; unable to discern the melody, like a thin thread, imponderable above the noise of the crowd. I stared at Judith standing there. After a while she bent forward, to throw a coin I guessed. She remained still again for quite a while before turning to come back across the square. She sat down and smiled at me.

"Did you hear? He plays better when one listens to him."

Was it my bad mood rising again?

"It's the money you gave him."

"No, it's not. He started to play better as soon as I stood beside him, before I threw my little banknote … "

"Then it was so you'd give it to him."

She turned towards me and I saw her laugh even before it burst.

"Perhaps you're right. I wanted to make him happy so much that I thought he was doing the same for me."

I looked at her and invented a much finer ear for myself than I really have:

"No, you're right. I did notice that he … yes, he had a better sound, more pliable."

We both laughed. Who believed who?

What followed happened almost immediately, without warning. She leaned towards me, her mischievous gaze turned slightly to one side, a slight smile on her lips:

"Excuse me … Did you … Have you seen that man there, on your right, slightly behind you?"

I understood straight away. Immediately, that sour point within, that the violin player had almost erased, rose once more in my throat. Without turning my head, I answered: "You want me to look at him … You mean, now? Or in thirty years time?"

The small cascade of her laugh glided over me:

"You do know Charles Millau's game?"

Did I know my uncle's game! … I nodded.

That was it. This time, uncle was officially established between us, no longer in my private doubts, nor in our parallel dialogues, but openly, named. He was sitting there, at this table, with her, with me, with both of us. In between us. I couldn't look at her any longer. She knew the game ... I should have thought of it. So? Questions began to whirl about my head. What did she know about me? What did she want to know? I forced myself to look at her, and my eyes fell on her greying hair. My uncle and Judith, it happened thirty years ago ... I was scarcely born ... I felt like an idiot.

I dodged the question, answering, with a certain nervousness in my voice:

"But it was not a game. My uncle never played games, neither bridge, nor chess, nor draughts. He detested all forms of games."

"What, he never played ... No board games, of course. He could barely recognise the cards in *The Cardsharp* by La Tour ... "

I knew that ...

"But his own game, his private game, was this one: looking at people."

I turned my head, I glanced at the Englishman. I could hear: "The nose, Pierre, look at the nose....." and I thought, how many times, uncle? Here, perhaps? You played here, 'played', as she said, at this terrace, at this table, under this parasol? I felt I was becoming jealous. I felt like defending myself.

"I'm sorry, no. I assure you. It was not a game, at least not what one calls an entertainment, a diversion. It was a very serious occupation of his mind, a certain way of looking, by stepping back in time.

"But it was a game. A serious game, if you like, a serious and even sometimes cruel game, but a game nevertheless. He smiled as he played it."

"No, I don't believe it. It was an intellectual exercise. By looking at people, he would make them enter history with him. He would look at the person at the next table … "

—I couldn't help glancing again at the Englishman—

" … with the astonished eyes of a contemporary of Urbino the Eighth or Lorenzo di Medici. That's why you thought he was smiling. It was the expression of his astonishment. How can one be so ridiculously dressed? Why is he not wearing a feathered hat? Why is he not carrying a sword? And his wife … "

"You see, you are playing too … "

"Not at all. I'm not playing. I'm looking from the depth of time at a man of today, and I find him ridiculous in his chequered shirt. And grotesque for not seeing how ridiculous he is. But my uncle used to do the opposite too. He transformed his neighbour into a Florentine citizen from the Quattrocento … "

"In one wave of a magic wand … "

I was losing my cool, I was lecturing and she didn't hesitate to interrupt me. I was annoyed, like a primary school teacher with a pupil who won't be quiet.

"And so he would gauge him as if there was three centuries between them, and both ways—looking at a man three hundred years later or imagining him three hundred years earlier."

I, stiff and scholarly. She, slightly dreamy.

"He used to screw up his eyes, smile and say: 'How strange men are … They find their thoughts obvious, they believe their small daily gestures are natural, little do they know … ' "

"Straight away, he projected his imagination into a point in the future exactly symmetrical to the past where he was: 'How stupid shall we look … ' "

Our eyes met. I said to myself: we are talking about

exactly the same thing. But is it really the same thing? I switched gear.

"Step out of time. Which means not to content himself with what he saw, but immediately to broaden the problem, or more precisely to set a problem, the core of the problem, starting with a detail of ordinary life, from the time of Vermeer or our time. That ability to step out of time was an incredible instrument, a tool."

She cut me short.

"One day, I was looking at myself in the mirror … He saw me … "

I lowered my eyes. He looked at her looking at herself in a mirror? I pondered: shut up, you idiot.

"He said to me: 'Imagine the world of women before mirrors existed. Mirror … fair mirror … ' He hummed. 'In the past, women were dependent on what they were told they were. They were as beautiful as they are today, but they only knew it through the gaze of men. The consciousness they had of their beauty was necessarily 'reflected', in inverted commas. It was a second beauty, a beauty at second degree. Now, they are beautiful at the first degree, by looking in a mirror which gives them a direct image. They have no more need of men.' "

"Even if it's for men that they are happy to be beautiful?"

"Yes, of course, but they control from the first. Your uncle used to say: 'The relationship between men and women changed when the mirror was invented.' He told me the history of the mirror. He spoke about Venice, about the trade and industry of the mirror, and insisted that something changed in the world because of Venice in the sixteenth century. Before the mirror, an old woman was an old woman, full stop. Then, at a certain point in history, she could no longer accept growing old in the same way. The mirror is responsible for all false beauties … "

"But don't you think that men's gaze deceived them too?"

"Obviously. And today they take in what they want from the image reflected in the mirror … "

Her laugh again …

"You see, it was all a game … "

I listened to the light trill in the shrill of her voice, gliding down like a mellow glissando, blooming in the deep notes, then spreading, letting go. I could hear deep within me my uncle's voice reciting the words of his little notebook: "Take me, I love being loved … "

"Yes, yes, I assure you … "

She had a way of pronouncing "I assure you" ("I a*ss*ure you") while looking straight into my eyes, which obliged agreement. I lowered my eyes. I tried to see myself, here, under the green-and-white parasols, seated next to my uncle, looking at people. But she resumed, and her voice suddenly changed.

"No, I exaggerate. The truth is that he was looking at faces as if they were painted. For him, they were not people, they were portraits. I mean, virtual portraits, potential portraits. A face was the material for a portrait. A portrait not yet made … And before some portraits, your uncle saw people—he was becoming a kind of novelist. He created stories … "

I stiffened. Still that little insidious anger held inside me. My uncle, a novelist? … I grumbled:

"He was also looking at the brush strokes … Actually, that is where his passion lay, finding the hand of the painter."

"Don't make me say what I didn't say. What I'm saying is that he used to look at people in the street as if they were their own portraits. The same person but, how to say it, not entirely finished, not fully constructed. The face of a living man or woman was a sketch, a rough draft. And, in the museums, on the other hand, he looked at portraits as if they were people, with their own stories. Faces finally completed ... "

I glanced once more at the Englishman. I tried to see him with the eyes of Uncle Charles. He was leaning towards his companion, whispering something in her ear. I needed to see his eyes in order to draw his mouth. Mouth and eyes are inseparable, my uncle used to say. They console each other, but sometimes they also contradict each other. They play the same part with different techniques: and then, that discord.The woman was laughing, with that little dry and retracted laugh some English women have. It would have been better if I had seen her, but she had her back to me and offered me only the reddish-blond, frizzy hair on her thick, pink neck.

"You mean to say that my uncle projected painted faces in time as he did with passers-by, that he invented a past for them and imagined a future?"

She didn't answer straight away, but looked at me for a few moments. My tension grew beneath her gaze, as if ...

"But, dear sir ... Can I call you Pierre?"

"On the condition that I call you Judith." She continued to look at me in silence. Judith ... It had been less than a hour since I started talking with her. What did she know about me? What did she know of what I knew about her? I didn't have the time to think any further. She was challenging me already.

"I just can't imagine, Pierre, that you have worked for so long with him and that you ... For how long?"

"Fifteen years. In a way, I continue ... "

And she, how long? The ten seconds of her focus on me were a judgement, an evaluation. I didn't have any numbers to offer. No, there was one. I was looking at her, and something deep inside me said to her: in the Jardin du Luxembourg, you could have had a three month old baby. You said it, he wrote it, I read it. But you don't know I read it.

"Fifteen years! And in fifteen years, he told you nothing? Not a single story?"

"I don't understand … "

"You never saw him in a museum, you … "

I roared with laughter, silently. What, me never saw my uncle in a museum? Every day, every day …

"You haven't seen the expression on his face in front of a portrait he was very fond of, I don't know, *The Little Girl with the Dead Bird?*"

"That one in the Brussels museum?"

If I wanted to show her that I couldn't be caught out so easily, even by citing a little known small painting by an anonymous artist, it failed. Her glance drove me into resentment, as if she was making fun of me. So what? Is there any other *Little Girl with the Dead Bird* than the one in the Brussels museum? Of course I have seen it, several times, Uncle Charles having stopped at length before that small Flemish painting that I knew moved him. He had remarked on the fineness of the pleats on the sleeve of that little girl with big sad eyes who holds a sparrow with a hanging wing in her hand. I can hear him still: "Look, Pierre, how he dissolves that Prussian blue on a background whose saffron he makes us guess at without really showing … What finesse … And all that to better frame the blue of her eyes … What skill … Who could have painted that picture?" I closed my eyes for a second and I saw him: serious, concentrating. Yes, it was true: moved, touched, deeply affected. Judith's voice reached me from far away, superimposed on Uncle Charles'.

"He christened her Margreet ... Margreet van something. Wait ... "

It was her turn to close her eyes, but with a smile as if, from what she was seeking in a hiding place in her memory emanated a foretaste of sweetness and charm, something she sensed before she could identify it.

"Here it is ... Margreet van Kleeneberg. That means 'the little mountain'. Your uncle invented that name and repeated it with amusement, exaggerating its Northern sonorities, as if to pretend some kind of old grandfatherly tenderness."

She repeated: "Margreet van Kleeneberg."

Never heard that name before. To me, my dear uncle didn't tell stories. He talked painting. I could feel myself becoming peevish as she carried on.

"He imagined her ... No, he didn't imagine her. He saw her old, as one could be at that time when one was fifty or sixty, with the same grey-blue eyes. But, he added: 'Look. She is five years old and already, she has old woman's eyes, with the lower lids drooping slightly through age. Already, already the beginning of that sagging at the corner of the eyelid.'"

There, I recognised exactly my Uncle Charles' technique. One takes everything one finds on a face and modifies it according to what one sees prefigures its future. Without thinking twice, I turned towards the Englishman, and almost laughed. What a face he was going to have ... And he didn't suspect anything. My eyes returned to Judith, and something surprised me in her expression. She was whispering: "Poor little one ... " It took me a while to understand. It was not her talking, it was my uncle.

"He looked at her with infinite tenderness and repeated: 'Poor little one ... ' He showed me her mouth, her tight little lips, closed on this incomprehensible cruelty of the world,

78

the death of a bird. First encounter with pain. I could hear him whispering: 'What, pain? What is pain?' He turned towards me and said: 'Look at her. She is five years old, and she refuses. Look at her mouth.' And I could hear him mumbling *'Neen. Neen. Neen.'* And then: 'It's not the mouth, it's the relationship between the mouth and the eyes.'"

Exactly what I'd just thought, a minute earlier.

"And then he showed me the softness of her round hands (he called them 'baby hands'), which held the dead bird carelessly, as if all the little girl's attention had shifted, had left the bird, to settle elsewhere, towards what she stares at with incredible concentration and steadiness. 'Look, look … ' and he pointed out the grey-blue eyes: 'Can you see?' He waited to see if I had understood. 'The painter has refused to lay down, with the tip of his brush, the little touch of light, the little sparkle one sees on every eye of every portrait of every painter of all times. Her eyes are smooth. Nothing to read.' He added: 'She is absent. She is not there. She has gone … ' Then he started to murmur her whole story. 'She had a beloved little bird. She used to watch it hopping about in its cage, she used to bring it its portion of seeds every morning and every evening. She used to fill, with the care little girls take in important matters, the capsule of water she hooked to the bars.' He carried on inventing: 'After each meal, she would pick up the crumbs on the table to bring to it, and when she ate, she pecked in her plate with her finger tips to imitate her bird, which was the charm, the life, the poetry of life, music, beauty, tenderness, love … On that morning, she screamed: *'Mama! Kleen Fifi is tood!'* I can still hear your uncle whispering *'Mama!'* with the exact tone of that child's anguish. He brought tears to my eyes, your uncle."

I was staring at Judith. Her eyes lowered. Towards what?

Her memory? Uncle? Uncle's voice? The painting? That day in Brussels? Uncle's tenderness for the little girl of the painting, whom he christened as if to make her his own daughter, his own grand-daughter? Or his tenderness for Judith, for a woman, a real woman, reflected, resonating in the little painted face? And me? Who was I, me, next to my uncle, in front of the same little painted face? 'Look, Pierre, that Prussian blue … ' Why was Uncle Charles talking to me about Prussian blue? And when I was there, at his side, what was he thinking of? Why did he never mention a journey to Brussels in his notebook? I listened to Judith recounting my Uncle Charles telling the story of Margreet van Kleeneberg, and I suddenly thought: is she inventing too?

I looked at her in line with the great fountain of Bernini, sparkling in the afternoon sun. She had lowered her head in the gentle shade of the white-and-green parasol which, accordingly, softened her features. She too was somewhere else, withdrawn into that story she had told me, whose every word she seemed to know by heart after twenty-five years. I repeated to myself: is she making it up? How can one remember all those sentences? Uncle Charles didn't tell stories. What he saw on a face he analysed with such finesse that he could decipher everything about a person. But he didn't add any anecdotes, he didn't tell fairy tales, he didn't create myths.

However, what Judith told me touched me, for it was true: the little girl with the dead bird was exactly how she described her and her tale touched me. I entered the story with—what? affection? The return of my emotion for a small painting I had loved, that my uncle had made me love? My uncle, not her.

She resumed, and I no longer knew who spoke, she, or my uncle.

"She doesn't cry. She stares at her mother, with dull eyes. Your uncle had christened her mother too: Anneke. Anneke, with all the kindness of a tender mother, tries to explain to Her about existence, life, misfortune, things that happen, forgetting. She tells her that she will take her tomorrow to the shop in Huidenvettersplaats to buy her a little yellow canary that's even prettier. It's hard to console, your uncle used to say. One overdoes it ... But Margreet opens her wide eyes and one sees, one reads, on her forehead, on her mouth, in her dull and wide open eyes, one can read that refusal, that she can't put into words, poor little five year old girl who knows nothing of life, but who is closing down a corner of her heart for ever. And your uncle carried on telling me the story of that unknown child on a painting by an unknown artist. When she is sixteen, she will get married ... You see, I know everything by heart ... When I left the museum that evening, I wrote everything down."

Interesting ... She wrote too ... This time I smiled at her.

"Me too, I used to write when I left the museums ... "
I refrained from saying, just in time: the Accademia. After having slowly plodded along, offering my arm to help him in his painful walk, across the bridges of Venice, coming out of the Accademia, I used to write. I have entire books of notes jotted down in the evening in my hotel room, with my uncle's sentences. But why, to me, did he only talk about the pleats in the sleeves and the delicate blending of the Prussian blue?

"You see, he invented all the details, but they were real details. He even invented the name of the man she was going to marry at sixteen, the nephew of the burgomaster, Jans ...

Wait ... Ver ... Verde ... "
I leapt up. I knew that name.

"Your uncle didn't just read their faces, you know. He read everything, transcribed, translated: clothes, jewels, head-dresses, the elegance of the pleats in the sleeves … "

Ah! Finally! He talked about that to her too …

"All that made him see clearly that at the age of sixteen she would marry the son of a leading citizen, and not the son of a shopkeeper or an innkeeper. It was written, do you understand? I mean, painted. The only thing left was to give the young man a name. Or rather that name came spontaneously to mind, for he moved in the concrete world of things, the daily, the natural, life. Where was I?"

She talked, I listened. But my thoughts had suddenly branched off. I rummaged in my memory, not knowing exactly what I was looking for. What had she just said? I stared at her. I don't know what she could read in my eyes. I remained silent. What I'm trying to say is the deepest part of me remained dumbfounded and I didn't understand why.

"You were telling me she was going to get married to the son of, no, the nephew of the burgomaster, Jans Verde … I'm not sure what else."

Memory is strange … For the moment, mine was com-pletely blocked, as if astonishment had instilled an immobil-ity, an inertia. I lowered my eyes and dug savagely into the emptiness deep within, not knowing what I wanted to find in there. Jans Verde … I felt a slight jerk of silent laughter as I made an unseemly play on words, and that was per-haps what set the machine in motion again. Even before I recalled the syllables of his name, I saw him, the tall, big-boned, red-headed man leaning next to my Uncle Charles in the storeroom of the Rijkmuseum in Amsterdam, laugh-ing his enormous rugged laugh. It was that laugh that gave me his name again: Jans Verdegans. He was so pleased to discover an etching with my uncle in which Rembrandt had roughly sketched himself laughing too, a hearty laugh about which one wonders (since one can't hear it) if it is funny, poignant, or clumsily touching. Verdegans ... My uncle had made of that large, merry museum curator's name a sort of swearword that he uttered with comic emphasis to underline that our disagreement was not that serious. He used to say, "Verdegans!", as one would say, laughing, "Gadzooks!" "Egad!". Eyes lowered, I uttered: "Verdegans!"

Judith started laughing:

"Yes, yes, Verdegans ... "

Then more softly, as if she too was connecting something personal:

"Your uncle laughed as he pronounced his name."

But I was forging ahead. So Judith didn't invent stories after all? What she told me was not born from her own imagination. It was my uncle who had borrowed the name of that big Dutch curator, had fashioned his own amusing swearword from it before attaching it to the son, no, the nephew, of the burgomaster he had invented as well.

"Your uncle was a novelist. I don't believe you, Pierre, when you say that in front of a painted face, or in front of a real face, he only kept up a little intellectual game."

I felt tormented. I couldn't accept her calling my uncle a novelist. She was besieging me with proof that he told her (her, not me) stories, with characters bearing names I knew. I shored myself up:

"In front of a portrait, in front of a face, he analysed, he even theorised, sometimes. He used to say: 'Faces change with age, but not profiles. Look at the profile ... ' "

"You are still making me say what I'm not saying. You are terrible, Pierre ... I didn't say your uncle didn't think and didn't reflect. I'm saying ... "

She looked at me and burst out laughing.

"I'm exaggerating too, you know… What I'm saying is that beyond, or rather with the help of his scholarly deductions, his subtle analyses, he fabricated destinies. He made up stories. He lived them. That's why he christened the people, to make them exist. The man with the glove, you understand, Pierre, he is somebody. Otherwise, why the gravity, the melancholy in his gaze? What is he thinking about? Be careful, it's not good enough to content oneself with giving a name to the girl he loves. The question is: what is the secret, the heavy secret of her soul? Margreet at sixteen, he could picture her smiling like any young bride on her wedding day. And later arranging the flowers on the table before the meal. And then when one of her new-born died (you see, Pierre, he recounted her whole life), Margreet will not know that the weariness she feels in her soul comes from the day she listened to Anneke, her sweet mother, explaining life to her while she held her little dead bird in her hands and something deep inside her whispered:

'*Neen, neen, neen* … ' "

She went silent for a moment, her eyes in the distance, or caressing the façade of Saint Agnes. Then, very softly:

"Your uncle was a very touching man."

I knew that. You only had to go beyond the slightly old-fashioned stiffness he affected, which his smiling courtesy permitted one to do in an instant, to discover, as she said, a very touching man. "Pierre, would you be kind enough to look in the file of the Royal Collection in London … " But why to me, why to me did he only talk about the fineness of the pleats in the sleeves and the subtlety of the creases in the shirt of the man with the glove? Why didn't he talk to me about his soul, and why didn't he tell the story of Margreet? Was I unworthy of receiving the confidence of his imagination? Was I nothing but a dry spirit, to whom one talks about technique and brush strokes? Or else is it good practice as a teacher not to lead a beginner off course with one's rigour and method? And what about a female beginner? What does one do with such a beginner, my dear uncle?

I raised my eyes again to meet hers, anger bubbling up, but stifled the moment mine caught the blue of hers. What if it was my uncle who had dried up?

Silence.

The blue of the eyes of the little girl with the dead bird. We had made the journey to Brussels to meet a very learned colleague. We were walking down the museum's main gallery. My uncle had stopped in front of the little painting, forty centimetres by thirty. "Pierre, look at her eyes. It's the only portrait I know where the painter has refrained from adding the little sparkle that all painters of all eras … " Blue eyes, but dead. What was Uncle Charles thinking about?

Was it my uncle who had dried up with age? Or else …

Silently, it was she to whom I spoke now:

Judith, when my uncle left you (he was the one who left, I do know that), did he abandon, as he descended the steps, suitcase in hand (he left like that, I know, leaving you alone in your hotel room in Venice), did he also abandon everything that was alive in him, the novelist, as you say, to leave me only the fine savourer of brush strokes? Is my uncle, the one I knew, the one I loved, the one who taught me everything I love, was he only a dried-up heart, a lonely soul who hid behind his smile? Was the ever-so engaging smile of my dear old uncle only a mask?

Impossible. When he talked about Simonetta, sweet, so sweet, what he said didn't come from a shrivelled heart. I looked up at her. My memory was working well now. "Pierre, the way she pronounces, you see? … The shape of her lips forces you to hear the sweetness of her Venetian lisp ... *O felici sospiri e degni pianti* ... " Kisses, for you uncle?

How long ago was it? Twenty five years? Thirty years?

I looked again at the grey hair, cut like a boy's, and suddenly, in a kind of dazzle, I saw her, her, Judith, leaning towards me over the table, her cheeks still broadened by her cascading laughter, as she was thirty years earlier, with slimmer cheeks, the same eyes full of laughter, but without the dark circles and without the small wrinkles around the eyelids, bigger, laughing but differently, in a lighter way, and her hair blond like all the gold of Danaë, laughing, laughing and shrieking with delight:

"Carpaccio, yes! Bellini, yes! Antonello da Messina, yes, yes!"

I must have had a funny look in my eyes. She stopped abruptly.

"Are you playing? I mean, are you playing with me?"

She started laughing immediately as she looked at me. I laughed too, without answering.

And it was then exactly that a young woman, very like the Judith I had just glimpsed, with the same face but longer, the same blue eyes but bigger, dressed in a white t-shirt and jeans, placed her hand on Judith's shoulder and leant down for a kiss.

"Hi, mum!"

Judith's round face beamed suddenly: her cheeks as she stretched sideways, looking up, her eyes whose laughter softened with her happy embrace, while her hand went around the neck bending towards her and stroked the blond hair.

It seemed I was already forgotten.

I had all the time I needed for contemplation while nobody thought about me. I had simply ceased to exist.

Two faces, so similar and yet completely different; and I unable to say how they resembled each other and how they were different, nor if one was the copy of the other, nor which was the original, for one seemed new and fresh, and exactly the same thing seemed more detailed, more elaborate and more finished in the other. Nose, mouth, cheeks: everything was there. It looked as if uncle's game (and there I was calling it 'the' game ...) had ceased to be a game of imagination and dreaming and was suddenly incarnated in two faces. This one, leaning towards the other and angled in profile to kiss it, and that one facing me but entirely absorbed in its elevating movement. Cheek against cheek: one fleshy and slim at the same time, against the other, similar but more fluid, more malleable, slightly whiter, lined by a large, tender furrow around her mouth. And the mouths: similar, both laughing, one pinker, firmer, still rounded and swollen by the movement of the kiss, at its extremities joining two dimples, in which I saw clearly (I was not guessing, not imagining: I saw) that into twenty years time, they would have hollowed and lengthened in those two wrinkles that encircled the other mouth, a bit purpler, a bit softer, and which was laughing too. And the two laughs: parallel, bound together in a barely audible counterpoint, almost immediately emerging as words.

"So, darling. How was it?"

"Super, Mum. I love it ... "

And in that "I love it," the uncle's voice again. "Take me, carry me away, I love being loved ... "

And only then, at that moment, Judith's eyes turned towards me, and her mouth announced with a kind of greediness:

"This is Sarah ... "

PART THREE

WHEN SARAH CAME TO LIVE with me, in that old house, that welcoming, considerate, rather solemn, old house that I had inherited from Uncle Charles, and which had probably never heard a single animated voice, and in which only the sound of the telephone ever resounded or, in the morning, the baritone voice of the postman in the hall: "Madam Mariette, I've a parcel for you," that afternoon then, the walls, the tightly packed bookshelves, the old polished furniture, the paintings, the drapes, everything must have trembled right up to the attic, like a three-master ship caught in a storm. Sarah landed with her apple green Citroën 2CV, her bags, her boxes of books, her computer, her duvet, and started whirling around with shrieks of delight.

"But your place is a castle! You didn't tell me!"

No, Uncle Charles' house was not a castle, but one of those large semi-rustic houses they used to build in the nineteenth century for families with eight children, plus the sister who never got married, and the widowed aunt whose husband had been killed in the Crimean war. The kitchen, with its big black stove bearing handles of shiny steel which hadn't been used for fifty years, was much too vast for old Mariette. The magnificent drawing-room which had received visits from the sub-prefects and perhaps even church dignitaries on their way to confirmation, had gradually been filled to the ceiling with books, and was only used for work, my uncle's and mine, and now just mine. Sarah ran everywhere, peering about and shrieking with happiness.

"And you live here all by yourself ? All this just for you? Lucky I've arrived! And that, where does that go?"

"The cellar … "

"Filled with sublime fifty year old bottles of Bordeaux layered in dust. Yeah. I'm gloating ... "

For the moment, what seemed to impress Sarah most were the paintings. She had stopped, mouth agape, in the middle of the library. I could see that her eyes, skating over the lines of books, had halted on the surfaces left free by the panels of the library, where Uncle Charles' favourite paintings, framed in gold, were hung on two, three, sometimes four levels. I looked at Sarah's surprise, her wide eyes, her broad smile of amazement, I mean, of naïve astonishment, as if having in one's house, in one's very home, real paintings like one sees in museums, provoked in her an explosive mix, yes explosive, that's really the right word, of incredulity, wonder, emotion. She talked to herself:

"It's not possible ... Not possible ... Look at that, just look ... I love it."

Those paintings were, however, neither Reubens, nor Van Dyck, nor Poussin and, except for one, they were not very big. They were beautiful works painted by unknown masters (not unknown to my uncle, of course), that he had purchased in auctions or from provincial antiques dealers, where his infallible eye had spotted them, and, above all, that he loved. And what touched me precisely in Sarah's amazement, what gave rise that evening and the following ones, to waves of tenderness, was that she could instinctively detect the unity of this rather haphazard assemblage of small paintings, which was precisely the love that the old man had felt for them. Yes, Uncle Charles, the passion for painting, as you said ...

On the left there was a small Virgin with a beautiful oval face and the soft, black and velvety eyes of a Spaniard, circled with a tender blue veil. Nothing, it was almost nothing, except that we had discovered it together, my uncle and I, one afternoon.

"Take a look, Pierre ... School of Murillo. One of his pupils, I don't know which. Perhaps Juan de Valdès, or Luis Salvador ... We'll see when it's cleaned ... "

My uncle had a special flair, a gift of instinct. He was like a water diviner who confirms, hazel stick in hand: "Just there you'll find water ... " In the jumble of a squalid bric-a-brac shop, amongst the heaped tables and the sunken armchairs, he went straight to the corner where twenty crudely-daubed paintings were stacked, and that's where he unearthed his little treasure. He used to wink at me and whisper:

"Go and look elsewhere, Pierre, while I negotiate. I want it for twenty francs."

Uncle Charles was not mean with money, he could barely count. But if discovering in a corner the work of one of Murillo's pupils was not already a joy he savoured and shared with me, to buy it then for a hundred francs was a double pleasure, which had nothing to do with money, not even with craftiness or the art of deception, but solely with that of the water diviner. ("I told you there would be water here."). Each of the paintings in the library, in the dining room, in the corridor, along the stairs, had its story, thus the charm of their anecdotes was added to that of the odd kind of fraternity which linked the paintings to each other. In their moulded gilt frames, they gave the impression one was entering a small, welcoming museum. On Sarah's face, in her surprised smile, in her twirls, I discovered something I'd never measured, of which I only ever had a weak, hasty awareness: yes, truly, my uncle, it was that, the love of painting.

"Tell me, is it really your uncle who put all those things there? Ah, I'm beginning to understand ... That man was somebody. And he left you everything?"

It was the first time Sarah had talked about Uncle Charles.

"Do you know my uncle?"

"Only because of Mum. She never stops talking about him. His name is always on her tongue. He was her god ... "

That's new.

"He was her teacher. I'm sure she was in love with him. Hey, do you realise that if Mum had married him, all this would be mine? Gosh! Why are you looking at me like that? You think you had a narrow escape? I don't care, you'll give me everything if I marry you."

She spun round, burst into laughter and continued:

"Wow, if I'd known all this was waiting! Everything at the same time: a boyfriend, a bit dumb but nice, a castle out of the Arabian Nights, a dream museum, three tons of old books, all wrapped up and ready to go. The first prize ... "

Her joyful screams overran each other when she entered the vast room that had once been the dining room, in which I'd seen my uncle take his meals until a few days before he died, all alone at the top of the big table with its dozen chairs, where he sometimes invited me after a long working day, for a dinner served by old Mariette. He wasn't eating much any more; picked at a few mouthfuls, drank half a glass of Bordeaux, though Mariette insisted on preparing him formal meals, lovingly cooked starters, main courses with vegetables, cheese, dessert and an infusion to finish with. This dining room, no longer used since his death, had taken on, through lack of use, and even more so than the rest of the house, the air of a museum.

"I can't believe it! I just can't believe it! Look at that, it looks like, I don't know ... "

She cast her head in all directions, her arms wide, approached, fell quiet, stepped back, laughed, looked.

"It's incredible. Three months ago I was an ignoramus. Mum kept boring me to tears with her History of Art with a capital H. Do you say a *h*, or an h? A *h*, that sounds funny. Now, since Rome, I love it. Love it. You put me in front of a painting, and I rejoice. Do you think it's because I'm in love?"

Was it because she was in love? What about me, watching her in all her joyous and rollicking ecstasy? Was it because I was in love that her outbursts in front of what my uncle had loved with such modesty and restraint sent me gusts of tenderness for her, for him. And he, is it because he was in love that what he called "the passion for painting" had flourished inside him? What about Judith? Is love capable of making you sensitive to something you would never have thought about, wouldn't have thought of being moved by? Or rather, when one falls in love, is it necessarily with the person one has no idea is going to set in motion one's secret depths of passion, carried inside un-thought-of? Does one guess with whom one must fall in love because he is the one, she is the one who is going to make you become what you wanted to be? Uncle Charles, who were you? And me, who am I?

Sarah was still flitting around like a butterfly, while I kept quiet.

Beyond the dining room, through a small red-tiled corridor with a copper fountain and basin still shining as the day they were bought on one wall—there was the kitchen. And that's where Sarah and Mariette met for the first time.

At the time of my uncle's death, amidst the countless worries I had to face, the notary, the inheritance, the tax man, the members of the Institute, the American academics, there was also the problem of Mariette. She was the same age as him, she had spent her life in his home, she had no other family than him, even less—not even a nephew. I was her nephew. I was her family. Like my uncle, Mariette was an exile from another time. Should I send her away? Where to? To one of those places for old people, where she would have been doubly exiled until she died? I let her keep her bedroom, I added a bit of money to the pension my uncle left her and of which she wouldn't spend a penny ; and in the vast kitchen planned two centuries ago for ten kitchen boys, whose tiles she polished and scrubbed while complaining about her back, she prepared my evening meal. She answered the phone when I was away: "No, monsieur Pierre is not home." She called me "monsieur Pierre" as she used to say "monsieur Charles" and grumbled when something disturbed the order established fifty years ago.

"Mariette, this is Sarah."

"Good morning, Madam," Sarah had said.

Nobody, probably, had ever called her "Madam". Scarcely ever "Madam Mariette", from the greengrocer when there was still one in the village, or from the postman whose punctuality she checked by the clock in the hall while drying her hands on her apron: "Good morning, Madam Mariette, I have a parcel for you. I'm not early today." But "Madam" alone, certainly not.

She had barely lifted her head from the green beans she was de-stalking.

"I thought I heard some noise … "

Noise? Sarah's laughter and shrieks of delight? Mariette had on her moody face.

"I wondered what was happening and who could possibly be screaming like that. My hearing is not very good but … "

"Mariette, Sarah is going to live here. We … "

This time, she lifted her head. She looked at me, then at Sarah. Her fingers carried on with their little task, over her apron, into whose hollow she let drop the tails of the beans she broke in two before throwing into a saucepan on a stool next to her.

"Sarah and I are going to … We are going to live together. I hope you two will get along fine. I'm sure you will. I … "

I looked at Mariette staring at Sarah with a curious look, attentive, deliberate, and my sentence came apart. I had expected the grumpy disapproval I saw in her eyes. I was even dreading it a bit. But there was something else. Mariette's hearing was bad, but her eyes were sharp, and she had no need to dwell on what she was looking at. It was later, much later, after Sarah left, that I understood.

For Sarah didn't stay at my house (at my palace, as she called it) more than six weeks. Forty-three days exactly: I had more than enough time after her departure to count them. She left on the morning of the forty-fourth day, the way she arrived, by surprise. Not once, ever, had I been able to foresee one of her decisions or one of her whims, no more than to anticipate one of her sallies, or to guess, sniff, imagine what her answer to one of my questions would be. She answered off the point. Her answers were indirect, roundabout, as if I had asked another question altogether. Or, on the other hand, they were so sharp, hit the target so exactly, that I couldn't have imagined, not even sensed their coming, and I would be pinned to the spot in amazement. As for her own questions, they didn't seem to follow what I had just said. She changed direction during my half-second silence, and I didn't have the time, before the next one, to realign my compass. Always caught unaware, but so well caught that my slowness, the succession of small emptinesses and little nothings which dug into my thought at each of her arrows, metamorphosed from one minute to the next into a succession of weightless joys born of the unexpected sparkle, the gracious pirouette, the rocket or the bite of her arrows. Each minute brought me a new unexpected reason to fall in love. And each time, of course, in love I fell. In the evening, when she had fallen asleep, and I then had some time for my own thoughts, after turning off the light, I would revisit the small pleasures of the day. I had thought that human beings usually experience love once, at first sight, and after that they live their love; while I had the privilege of experiencing love at first sight every minute and didn't have the time to savour what poets call the delights of love.

That morning, I had risen early. Of all my old habits, this was certainly the only one she hadn't managed to modify. She had transformed my meals, (dear old Mariette indignant, disgusted, but silent) into picnics on the lawn, in front of the terrace where Uncle Charles used to take his coffee in summer. She had re-organized my office within twenty-four hours, swapped the tables round, set up her computer in the place where for fifteen years I had seen my uncle work, and where his ink pot, his blotting pad, his tobacco tin and his ashtray had remained since his death, exactly where he had put them. She had fetched a pedestal table from the dining room, to gather those relics together, henceforth exiled to a corner. She had undertaken to convince me that my documentation had to be computerised and that my precious index cards dated from before Gutenberg. She threaded her way into my vocabulary, changing my words, damaging my syntax. Instead of reading in my bed, at night time, I caressed a woman's body, contemplated her face, the softness of her closed eyelids, unable to bring myself to turn off the light.

But Sarah's capacity to turn everything upside down as soon as she appeared was not operational in the morning. She hadn't managed to keep me in bed except for the first few days. In truth, at that time of day she was quite power-

less. The strength of her sleep, the heaviness of her leth-
argy were proportionate to the lightness of her waking, and
from one to the other there was no period of transition. She
talked to me, laughed, asked me a question and before I had
time to finish my answer, there was nobody there to hear
it and I was talking to myself. In the morning, eyes closed
(could I ever decide what I liked best, her eyes open, her angled glances, always direct like arrows, or her eyelids closed
beneath her brows, as soft as caresses?), her lips, swollen and
pressed against her closed fist, when I brushed them lightly
with a kiss before going out, she whispered, "I'm asleep".
And it was true, she was sleeping. Even better, she seemed to
take the opportunity of the small disturbance that, despite
all my care, I had caused while climbing out of bed, to become aware of her sleep and thus to cherish it even more.
Her "I'm asleep" was a profession of faith.

Each morning I had crept across the bedroom, bare-foot,
slippers in hand. I had closed the door slowly, controlling
the handle in case it creaked. I had slid into my slippers
on the landing and descended to the kitchen. Mariette was
still asleep at that hour, her cat likewise. I was the only one
awake in the house, as it had been every morning at that
hour for years. I had prepared a cup of coffee, the only
thing Mariette allowed me to do, for reheated coffee is never
good, she said. "Monsieur Pierre, if you want to drink your
coffee before I'm up you will have to make it yourself. At my
age, I need my sleep." I used to drink my coffee standing or
walking around the kitchen, then I would sit at my table and
start to work. I knew that in two or three hours' time, even
later sometimes, the door would open very softly, noiselessly,
and that Sarah would enter, exactly as in the painting I
liked above all others. Sometimes a towel around her waist
like a loincloth or sarong, but more often, nothing at all, as

incongruous and familiar in the doorway of Uncle Charles' office as if the real Botticelli Venus had entered in person, pretending, like his model, to hide her breasts with her hand, rosy like her, her eyes dreamy like hers, still brimming with the sleep she hadn't yet quite finished.

"You're already up, my love? I don't understand how you can … What time is it?"

And then with the mock sulky tone of a Botticellian nymph:

"I'd like us to have a real lie-in one of these days. The two of us. You would bring me a tray with croissants, you would lie down again and play the baker until midday."

Baker was my title, my function. We hadn't been slow to discover the precise nature of our pleasure before sleep. She lay down on her front, head on crossed arms, eyes closed, her back surrendered to my hands. How can I say whose pleasure was the greatest? That of my fingers, my palms, or that of her back, her neck, the small vertebrae I climbed step by step and went down again with the index and middle finger, in quick time or instead swaying and hobbling, or with my palm kneading slowly and deliberately on her velvety hips, powerfully sculpting her shoulders, moulding her curves, massaging, working, until one night, without opening her eyes but with, in her whispered voice, a kind of exuberance which would have proved to me, if needed, how wide awake and alive she was in that apparent somnolence, she had exclaimed with a fake Provençal accent:

"Oh, Baker!"

I had laughed, not really understanding. I had sensed the joy in her tone, but my slowness had only grasped a pleasant allusion, Orane Demazis addressing Raimu in an old film by Pagnol. She had to repeat it:

"Oh, Baker!"

Then, with a little laugh at the back of her throat, and that accent still:

"Am I a good dough?"

God, how slow and dull-witted I was!

"I'm rising! I'm rising! Can you feel your dough rise, Baker?

Don't stop!"

And so it was, Baker had become my name and all the metaphors of bread and pastry making, our intimate language, were wrapped in a Provençal accent.

When I saw, or rather guessed, perhaps because of a slight noise on the stairs which would have brushed across my mind and made me look up, when I sensed the door was about to open, I felt a little breath of happiness rise that I had been awaiting for two hours while pretending not to think about it. Having drunk my coffee, I sat at my table, opened a file and started to work. That moment of solitude, each morning, was the only one which still had some resemblance to what I could call my life before Sarah. I was back, not only to my usual occupations, but to a rhythm, a quietness in the way my thoughts followed each other, a softness of the silence, which plunged me right back into my way of life, yes, that's it—of before Sarah. I examined the fine scratches on a drawing by Sebastiano del Piombo that I hadn't been able to see in Rome because of my desertion of the learned conference, and whose reproduction I had had sent. I was wondering about its links with a fresco in the Villa Farnesina, questioning whether my learned colleagues had thought about it. All my habits had returned to their old rhythm. Of course, it was an illusion. In the background of Sebastiano, as an imperceptible counterpoint to the happiness of breathing the air of the Farnesina, a kind of mist floated, gently framing my thoughts, a separate haze of contentment, sweet, peaceful too, born from that closed door which I knew sooner or later was going to open, by surprise—wonderfully—by surprise. That is habit too. One gets used to anything, even the unexpected. I was learning this from the daily, but still unpredictable repetition of this strange, unlikely apparition of a naked young woman in the austere working place inherited from my old uncle, in which I too perpetuated his routine. I was learning that habits, if they plane and file pleasure, can also make it a uniform material on which exquisite little delights can be grafted in relief. I worked, thinking about nothing beyond Sebastiano del Piombo's drawing and the fresco of Polyphemus at the Farnesina, not knowing what I admired most: their beauty, or my astuteness at having guessed that one was the preparation for the other. But I worked on in the pleasant aura of a silent happiness, smooth and unctuous, born from the silent wait for the subtle sound of the lock, the movement of the door as it opened and those words: "You're up already, my love?"

The door opened. I looked up, smiling. Sarah appeared, fully dressed: t-shirt, jeans, sandals, and her hair tied back in a pony tail, instead of the golden and frizzy morning halo. Her hair surprised me even more than the clothes. And in my surprise, I was the first to speak.

"Sarah! What's happening? You're dressed?"

For the first time, it was me who asked:

"What time is it?"

She didn't reply. I looked at my watch.

"Ten o'clock? And already dressed!"

As she walked towards me, the light from my window, facing my table, touched her face. There I discovered her drawn features, a stiffness in her mouth and in her eyes, that sleep hadn't blurred as other mornings, something I couldn't read.

And her voice:

"Pierrot, I think it's better like this. I have to go."

Of course, I didn't understand.

"But where are you going?"

"I'm leaving."

"To do what?"

"I didn't sleep last night. I've been thinking."

Didn't sleep, Sarah!

Amidst the confusion her last words had just planted in me, the incomprehension, the perplexity, and a faint dread grew. A desire to laugh insinuated itself too, as if she had just staged a prank. Sarah, not sleeping! She hadn't moved, nor blinked, nor twitched a finger since the moment when, before turning off the lamp, I had gently touched her with a last caress and she had whispered in an already misty breath: "Sleep well, my love, sweet dreams … ", while I contemplated once more the face on which sleep had already placed its velvety mask. I was about to start laughing, thinking about that, when she cut me short:

"Yes, I've been thinking, you see. It's better like this. I'd better leave. Since we had an argument … "

That's when I jumped.

"Had an argument? When did we have an argument?"

I still had the remains of my laughter lurking within, which hadn't had a chance to burst out. Bits of it were mixing now with my confusion. And she, suddenly stiff:

"You don't even remember? So that's all it does to you? I'm telling you: you and me, we're light years apart. You see, it's not that you're awful, besides, I love you, but what I'm feeling leaves you cold. You don't even remember it … "

I made an effort to remember our discussion of the previous night, but it was only a very long time after her departure, long after the purr of her Citroën had ceased to resonate in my head, that I managed to glimpse what was happening in hers. At the last moment, she had turned back, dropped her travel bag and buried her face in my shoulder:

"Forgive me, my Pierrot. I do like you, you know. I'll phone you. I don't feel like leaving you. Besides, I'm not leaving you. I just want to breathe for a while. Are you angry with me for what I said?"

She had added:

"Think about it. You'll see, I'm right."

And then, as suddenly, without looking at me, she had picked up her bag and left.

I hadn't found the strength to accompany her. I had remained in the hall, heard the buckled sound of her Citroën's bent door, the spluttering of the starter, once, twice, a third time yes, as if her friendly old car hesitated to obey and didn't feel like going either. And then, the big roar of the motor, angry under her foot. And then, decrescendo, until silence. And then, in the silence, the sound of Sarah's words. Argument. Argument. "You don't even remember?" When did we have an argument? A long time afterwards, seated at my table, my fingers resting on Sebastiano del Piombo's drawing, the sound of her joyful, agile voice floated around me.

"I don't get it. How can you say stuff like that?"

What for me was a discussion had been an argument for Sarah. And God knows we had had discussions, brisk and fast as her retorts, during those six weeks: about the house, life, the place of things, about meal times, Mariette, Rome, world history, Russian literature, society, education, politics, about me, and about her. But as soon as we became heated, as soon as I tried to convince her that I was right, it was no longer a discussion. It was an argument.

"I don't get it. How can you say stuff like that? Your

Matthias Grünewald, of course he's German. So what? The German Soul. Yeah. Jewish sensitivity. That's real racism. Not all German people think the same way… "

"But Sarah … "

"You talk about Wagner as if the whole of Germany has to fidget as soon as one hears *pam, pam, palam, pam, pam* (she started to sing the Valkyrie, but as one hears it at the cinema, in that film, what was it called?). That's all finished, my dear. You're behind the times. Those old theories, once again it's your uncle who's filled your head with them."

"But Sarah, listen to me … "

"I can't stand your uncle any longer. He put your brain in a cage."

It was with all her energy that Sarah entered a discussion. We had them ten times a day, every day. They were bright, jolly, happy, even when they became excitable. Her vivacity, the quick-fire bullets of her retorts had a capacity to lure me out of my own rhythms. I spent my time giving her masterful lessons, conferences, homilies to which she listened with an expression of delight on her face that made me swell up with a delicious mixture of tenderness and self-satisfaction. What is more beautiful in the world than what I felt then: to be a Pygmalion in love, scattering daisy seeds and seeing them blossom on the face of the woman he loves, to blend all one's proud knowledge with the memory of those kisses, caresses and whispers? All the subjects which constituted my life, my whole life, my only thought, my only occupation, my passion: beauty, art, I spread them on her like a sun lotion, and I delighted in doing so. Suddenly, with the vivacity and joyfulness of her heart, she threw in her grenade and exploded my calm along with my rhetoric.

"But, Pierrot, you say it's a masterpiece. Okay, if you want.

But I have the right to dislike it, no? So, it's a masterpiece for you, not for me. What is a masterpiece?"

I had to go back to my definition of a masterpiece. And even before the argument had time to get organised, to position its battery, in the middle of my exposition, everything came apart.

"But, goodness, you're talking like Hegel! Listen … " She sprang up, rummaged in her things, brandished a book with a smile of jubilation and examined it with total concentration, as she leafed through.

"Wait a minute, you'll see. I swear … "

I looked at her neck with tenderness. She sat up, in a halo of triumph and recited extracts from her philosophy course.

"I'm surprising you? At the Lycée, I was quite good. I even felt a bit guilty 'cos I used to see my mates slogging away like mad, pale-faced, talking shop between lessons. I did no work and got the best marks. The world is unfair. Yeah, I'm not stupid. But them neither, so what?"

Pretty quickly, I got used to Sarah's disordering of my life. I had taken a liking to the necessity of being on the alert every second, ready to face the unexpected, from the slipper standing all by itself in the middle of the carpet (and my eyes searching for the other one, but never finding it), to the question nothing allowed me to foresee (quick, the answer …), to the book I had put there, I was sure of it, and which was no longer there (but I'm not mad, I did put it there. "Sarah! Have you touched the book that was there on the table?"), that I even came to like it, desiring it, waiting for it without being able to foresee the particular pleasure which might turn up any minute. I, Pierre, the assistant crack-pot, it might be that after six weeks of this hubbub and debacle, I had loved Sarah for the chaos she brought into my house, my life and above all, my head. For it was the transference into things and into thoughts of the joy in her soul. The objects (one evening, Sarah: "But my Pierrot, inanimate objects have a soul, he said so, but they don't have legs!") were nothing compared to the disorder she infused into me, and of which I became aware when the Citroën's backfiring had ceased to reverberate, not in my ears, but long afterwards, in my head. The sound of the Citroën, that was another of Sarah's tricks, the absolute, radical surprise. The silence that followed, what was … it? Simply silence.

The sound made by Mariette as she came down the stairs brought me back to my senses. She knocked against the bars with her broom handle, all the bars, one after another, as she cleaned each step. It was the sound of the morning. To hear it confirmed that everything was fine, and, by distracting my ear for a second, signified that things were in order, that there was no place for dust in the world, that life, time, eternity, being, nothingness, the categorical imperative, everything was following its course. Mariette? I had forgotten her.

I looked down and stared once more at Sebastiano del Piombo, the profile of a man with a thoughtful air, who seemed not really to look at what he was looking at, and I thought, without thinking about it: "Like me, just like me." Then I repeated aloud, "just like me". I took hold of the photo, tore it, screwed up the bits and threw them into the waste-paper bin with a "ciao!".

Almost in the same movement, I plunged my hand back in, recovered the crumpled ball of paper and smoothing the sheet with my palm readjusted the pieces and continued talking to myself:

"Do you have a problem?"

Then, with a kind of chortling laugh:

"I'm talking like Sarah now."

I didn't remember getting up. But I paced up and down, talking:

"What is it supposed to mean: I speak like you, uncle? You have some nerve, telling me that my uncle put my brain in a cage. What is it supposed to mean? I'm not in a cage. I do as I please. If I hadn't known my uncle, what would I be now?"

I was holding the tobacco tin belonging to Uncle Charles in my hand. I had collected it from the little table where, six weeks earlier, Sarah had cast it into exile.

"You annoy me now."

I don't know whom I was talking to. Probably me. I placed the tin on the table, in its rightful place, then walked again the length of the library with the idea, I think, to fetch the ashtray which, when my uncle was alive, was always placed next to it. That's when Mariette came in.

"Miss Sarah … Her cupboard is wide open … It's empty. She took all her possessions? Has she gone?"

Ashtray in hand, I had my back to her. I didn't answer. What could I possibly have said? I cannot define the exact tone with which Mariette resumed: ironic? maternal? scolding? emotional?

"Poor monsieur Pierre … "

I was about to turn round. I had to say something. But she didn't leave me time.

"I didn't overly like her manners, but she was nice … Just like her mother."

When a thought, an idea, a sentence, a word, grabs me roughly, it hollows a black hole in me that I have to fill before my circulation and neurons can begin to function again. I have a word for that: flabbergasted. It suits me. It fits me like a glove. I was flabbergasted.

I took the time to turn and look at Mariette in the doorway, broom in hand.

"Her mother? You knew her mother?"

She emitted a laugh like a sleigh bell, resting both her hands on her broom.

"If I knew her … It's been a while, but I haven't had too much trouble putting things back my way … She was the only woman who entered this house, except for me of course. They were always arguing, monsieur Charles and Miss Judith. All the time."

Arguing? Uncle Charles? I mumbled, under my breath: "What is she talking about?"

"It made a terrible racket in the house. So, you know, Miss Sarah wasn't here a minute before I knew where she came from. I didn't need to look twice. I said to myself: well, monsieur Pierre is really following in his uncle's footsteps, like a kitten behind its mother."

At that moment, after six weeks' delay, I finally understood Mariette's look on that first day when Sarah entered the kitchen. Mariette looked at Sarah and saw Judith! I would be spared nothing. Nothing. She was smiling now, looking at me:

"Poor monsieur Pierre … I've bad hearing, but I can tell you that when I heard you arguing with Miss Sarah, I sometimes felt like laughing. It's starting all over again, I thought. And those two, they're young! So, she's gone? I think I'm going to miss her, despite the mess. Poor monsieur Pierre, you're going to miss her too. Poor monsieur Pierre …"

She looked at me, nodding.

"Wait a minute, I'll make you some coffee."

She turned to leave, but I stopped her.

"But Mariette, why didn't you say anything to me?"

"And what would I have said? I asked myself, where on

earth did he find that little one? But then you didn't say anything to me either."

She turned round and took upon herself to close the door.

I sat at my table again. Uncle Charles' tobacco pot lay before me. I looked at it. For years I had left it in its place, until Sarah arrived to disturb it. I lifted its blue china lid. A few crumbs of old tobacco remained at the bottom. I took them in my hand and lifted it to my nose. No smell. Nothing. And then, when I closed my eyes, for a moment, something from far away, an almost imperceptible after-smell, sweet, honey-like and rasping at the same time. Was it my nose smelling, or my memory inventing a keepsake? I put the lid back on the old pot (china from Bavaria, eighteenth century), slowly, holding the tiny handle between my index and my thumb. Lid. Uncle, Mariette, Judith, Sarah. Does the confined perfume resist time? In a notebook, yes. Shut in. Everything was closing up and adjusting itself in the minutest detail. So, Uncle Charles had arguments. Arguments, or discussions? I started laughing. Never, never, ever did I hear from his mouth one word spoken louder than another. His words were like his writing: a letter, then another, a word, a space, another word, a line, and in an absolute, definitive and perfect correctness, underneath, the next line, nothing excessive.

I opened the drawer, took out his notebook to look once more at the trace of his hand on the paper. I flicked the pages under my thumb, picking up on words *Scuola di San Rocco, San Zaccharia, Rezzonico*, and that sentence I didn't need to read, the one which had crossed my memory in that vaporous, musical, beyond-words way that old sentences, old proverbs, or old poems one used to know by heart and haven't recited for ages, have: *I will never return to Venice ...* And then under my thumb, the blank pages appeared, the ones on which my uncle had written nothing. I took my fountain pen and started to write on the first of those white pages.

Uncle Charles,

Is it true that you imprisoned my brain? I can no longer touch Sarah's memory without this sentence, uttered by her, coming back to my mind. Besides, the brain in a cage, what's that supposed to mean? That I can no longer think and that it is you who prevents me? What about Sarah?

My golden jail, my prison of love?

You see, my poor uncle, I can only write foolish things, I am desecrating your little notebook. If I had ever said something so stupid in front of you, you would have looked at me silently, from over your glasses, and I would have deciphered your smile perfectly: 'Think for a moment, my dear.' I knew all the nuances of your smile. Besides, I would have noticed immediately a slight retraction of your lips, which would have meant: 'Moreover, Pierre, speak properly.' For, you used to say, one can afford a momentary derailment of thought; but of grammar, never.

Look at what I've become, uncle. I start to write, I think I'm being serious, (Oh, I am, I am terribly serious this morning, believe me), but as soon as I have penned two lines, I start to mess about. I dodge. I skive, I elude. I take another long way round when I sense that I'm about to think. Terrible, no? You are right: I'm starting to speak like Sarah, since she left. For she left, my uncle, she is no longer here. What does that mean, brain in a cage? Does one die from being in a cage, like the bird of the little girl you christened Margreet, and whose name you never told me? And why didn't you tell me? Did you think I was too slow, or too stiff, or too blinkered to understand you? I don't know if I was imprisoned but you, why did you hide so carefully from me?

Oh, I can see you back then, Uncle Charles. You talked to me end-lessly about the Chardin blue, you discoursed on the way that old man, with his spectacles and his white cap, spread his blue and dissolved it into the entire space of his painting. You told me: 'Look, Pierre, there is blue everywhere, right up into the brown background, right up to the pink cheek of the school mistress, right up to her blond hair.' And I listened to you and admired you. Are you going to tell me that I didn't understand anything? It was by listening to you that I acquired the religion of the Chardin blue. I drank your words. 'A word, Pierre, like any masterpiece, exists only if someone listens to it. There are as many Fifth Symphonies as there are listeners. They can be grandiose or ridiculously narrow. Beethoven can't do anything about it. The greatest orator in the world has only ever pronounced the words that the most foolish of devotees at the foot of the rostrum could understand. The rest is wind.' Were those words addressed to me? What did I understand, when you talked to me? You talked about The Return from The Market. *Yes, I could see the woman in her blue apron. And the blue dress of* The Young School Mistress *in front of which you kept me in suspense for such a long time on that sad winter afternoon that we spent shivering in the National Gallery. You were lyrical. But about what? Lyrical about the Chardin blue? That's what I thought. You told me about the dialogue between the blue and the deep brown. 'How is it possible?', you kept saying. 'And that white, which is not white, but the apparition, the revelation (and in your lyrical élan, you said in Greek 'the epiphany') of all secret colours which, besides, are saturated with themselves. God invented white, and Chardin is his prophet.'*

There you are, uncle, I've found you again. I'm speaking like you now, without any errors of grammar. I transcribe your sentences in your notebook and I feel touched simply writing them, at the memory of your smile, your wisdom, your love of beautiful things and of Chardin's blue. Did I truly understand what you said? Or am I only a narrow-minded devotee at the foot of the rostrum, who understood only the superficies and sucked dry the meaning so as to shrink it to the size of his mind? Is The Young School Mistress *nothing but a dialogue between blue, white and brown, or do I have to christen her and invent a story for her?*

Forgive me, uncle. I'm still messing about. It's your notebook that brings back those moments when we talked painting and I was happy.

Sarah has left me and I am unhappy. What can you reply to me? For Sarah is not only gone. She departed accusing you. You. Why did she leave? Because we had arguments? You know perfectly well that's not the case. Besides, you did the same. But Judith didn't leave you: you left her, you. You wrote it yourself. What are you complaining about? The suffering that emanates from these pages I read touches me all the more because it surprised me, because you didn't let anything show or because I was too rough, or too naïve, or too light, insignificant, superficial, to guess it. But whom do you blame, uncle, do you blame? What are you complaining about? You loved painting for one month. I can find the page that's written on in ten seconds. Why one month? Who wanted it that way?

Uncle, I don't understand a thing. I don't understand any longer. I saw you in your last days. I saw you on your hospital bed, the one I didn't know, I didn't guess would be your death bed. Never, not once, did you talk about your death. No more than you talked about your suffering. You emanated a kind of peace, which I thought was from your soul. But I can no longer know what was in your soul. I didn't see you die. But I saw your death in the eyes of that blond nurse who reminded you of those Flemish portraits you liked, and with which you gave me your last lesson in Art History. You had moved her precisely because of your serenity, that quiet gentleness which you emanated a quarter of an hour before you closed your book and placed your glasses down to die. Where did you hide the pain that I read in the pages of this notebook, of which you showed nothing, neither on your face nor in your words? When you closed your book and placed your glasses down at the end of your chapter, did you still think you had wasted your life? Judith loved you, uncle. Thirty years later, she still loves you. Why did you let her have the child of another man? I don't understand. Sarah left me, and as she did she judged you. Accused you.

I am angry with you, uncle, for you put my brain in a cage and I don't know what that means. You have wasted your life? Tell me: Am I wasting mine? Somebody looking at me now, and who had learnt from you how to look at a face, could he tell me what I would be in thirty years time? Is it written on my face, here is the one who failed his own life? What can one read on my face? What am I now? Yesterday I knew. No, I thought I knew. Slight difference. There are four pages left in your notebook, uncle. It's not much. And the graphologists? What do the graphologists say? What does my writing have in common with my uncle's? Fifteen years of deciphering his spidery hand. That made my task so much simpler. Never a word in front of which one could hesitate, never a letter which overshot, never a question to ask. Everything was obvious, distinct, clear. And what do I understand? Nothing. I look at Judith with bewilderment. 'Do you know The Little Girl with the Dead Bird? *She is called Margreet.' So what? 'But Pierre, you haven't understood anything. Your uncle was a novelist.' Yes, I know, a very touching man, you told me so. What about me, for god's sake, me? Listen, Judith, I am in the process of ransacking my uncle's notebook because of your daughter, your nice little Sarah, who left two hours ago without telling me why, and not because of arguments. Mariette knows everything there is to know about the arguments, and you too. So bugger off. I'm not going to ...*

Mariette came in, carrying a tray, a cloth over her arm.

"Here's your coffee."

She looked to the right and left, pretending nothing was the matter, and placed the tray down on my table.

"There's no point worrying yourself sick, monsieur Pierre. Ah! Women ... They can cause so much pain without realising it ... monsieur Charles, when Miss Judith left him ... "

"Listen, Mariette, don't talk to me about all of that now. And, by the way, it wasn't Judith who left my uncle, it was him."

She had looked kindly upon me as she walked across the room carrying the tray and my cup, and even the little biscuits she had added to soothe my suffering. My last words took her by surprise as she lent towards the table. She stood up straight.

"What do you mean, him?"

Her eyes were indignant, with a violence I think I never saw before.

"And tell me, how do you know that? You were not here."

"Right, listen Mariette, please, leave me alone for a while. I don't feel like talking. Thanks for the coffee, it's very kind of you."

She left the room, mumbling something. She closed the door energetically and said, from the other side, loud enough to be certain that I heard: "He at least, spoke to me politely."

Even Mariette hated me.

I closed the notebook. If there had been a fire in the grate, perhaps I would have burnt it.

PART FOUR

IT WAS DURING THE LONG, ENDLESS symposium on History of Art at the Neue Pinakothek in Munich that I weighed things up. I went there with, I understood once there, a burst of what one calls reason, and which in fact was only my habits, leanings, taste, the well sign-posted paths of my daily thought. Everything was there to interest me. And when the professor from the University of Heidelberg announced, then demonstrated, how he was able to determine with certainty the identity of the *Woman in the Black Coat* in the Vienna museum, I believed for a moment I was about to recover my old passion. He had a way of relating his discovery, like a kind of Hercule Poirot, presenting each hypothesis as if it were true, certain, definitive, only to demolish it straight away and replace it with another, which he would reduce to nothing before reaching his conclusion. Yes, gentlemen, the woman with the black coat, is the same woman as the Magdalene of *Noli me tangere* in London, as the standing woman in the *Concert champêtre* in the Louvre ... For one moment, thanks to that academic doubling as detective, I felt pleasure at finding myself amongst these colleagues met so many times in Vienna, Rome, St Petersburg, Washington, London, all smiling, polite, pleasant, speaking amongst themselves with all the competence imaginable, some of whom had become almost friends. We talked about the things we liked, we offered each other little shared pleasures, we exchanged little signals of complicity ("Don't repeat it, my dear friend, I'm telling you this confidentially. I'm on the track of a great find ... Guess what ... "). In the past, my uncle had shone amongst them.

But very quickly I had fallen back into my inertia. My

mind was still in tow, not indifferent, but numb. Immediately, boredom broke in, soon, gradually turning into irritation. For no reason, something contracted inside me. This scholarly gathering of art connoisseurs, this tribunal of peers in which my uncle was admired and where I had enjoyed listening to people praise him, where I had started myself to be noticed, appeared like a remote world, as if a muffling screen separated me from it. The whole scene unfolded in front of my eyes like a bad film telling me a story I didn't believe in and, gradually, filling me with bitterness.

On the second night, instead of accompanying my colleagues to one of those Munich restaurants where it is almost impossible not to be caught up in the merry atmosphere and jolly mood, I took refuge in my hotel room. I watched German television and fell asleep, disgusted and bored, without reading a single line of the book I'd brought with me.

On the last day, I pushed my bitterness so far as to invent a false reason for not taking the same train as my colleagues returning to Paris. The thought of being imprisoned in the same compartment for several hours, without one minute when I would not have to smile, to answer questions, to pretend (pretend what? to be happy? to be joyful? to be friendly?) was unbearable. I wandered around for a while in the old quarters between the Marienplatz and the Frauenkirche, waiting for the next train, and then did what was inevitable in that city, I entered a tavern, noisily cordial and smoke-filled, where I was brought one of those enormous tankards full of Spring beer, the kind one drinks in Munich while laughing loudly with friends. I was the only one alone.

The very first mouthful of Maibock, rough, sharp, bitter, violent, revealed the truth about myself. It was I, I alone, deep down inside who was sour. It was I who was acrimonious and acid. "Rancid", I muttered under my breath. I swallowed a few gulps of beer and started to laugh when I realised that I took pleasure in this venom. I raised my tankard to eye-level and my eyes met those of my neighbour. I told him, without saying a word: "Look at me, man, look how unpleasant I am", and I started to unfurl in my head the procession of scholars, the important ones I had lived next to for four days, and I splashed them with my bitter beer. Poor old sods. They came one after the other to the platform, clad in their knowledge, fortifying one after the other the minuscule territory of their elite expertise, defending with tight smiles against the possible incursions of their colleagues, the cabbage patch, the real estate, the reserved district where they were privileged with immunity. I could hear them. "My dear friend, how can you declare that this drawing by Sebastiano del Piombo is really the one he presented for the triptych project of San Giovanni e Paolo, when I have demonstrated (demonstrated!) three years ago that this painter was absent from Venice at that date?" "But my dear fellow, if Lorenzo Lotto painted this picture in 1500, and not in 1506, that will force us to reconsider the entire first part of his career, and one can't do that, not at all, you say so yourself, for lack of any reliable document … " I swallowed another gulp of strong beer and sneered silently, repeating again and again, I'm the nasty one. I looked at those people as if they were puppets, ridiculous things. But who was the puppet? I was the one who was unsociable, impossible to live with, disagreeable, unbearable, intolerable. And I stupidly started to recite a litany of adjectives ending with able, capable, yes, capable of accounting for my pitiable, yes, pitiable deficiency. And then: What's happening to me? What am I? I emptied my tankard, stood up, said to my neighbour, who was still looking at me: *"Au revoir, monsieur,"* in a loud and clear French, and departed.

The drowsiness of that train journey I had wanted alone, only transformed my bitterness into a weariness of mind, body, and hands, which drummed on the book I didn't open. In fact, I didn't think. Impulses went through me, brushed me lightly and evaporated without my even trying to pin them down. I ended up falling asleep for real, as if I was tired of living. The automatic door of the carriage awoke me with a start, and what came to my mind proved that I hadn't stopped thinking while I slept. "What will become of me if what I loved, what has been my life, my only life, if even painting and the beauty of art no longer interest me? I am nothing." Then, awake: "Of course I'm going to carry on working. It's my job. I used to do it well, but … but what?" Silence. "Have I been on the wrong track for twenty years? Did Uncle Charles fool me?" "Pierre, will you file this note in the dossier marked 'Van Dyck in Genoa'. Thank you, Pierre … " So many years. What was it, happiness?

I loved my old uncle. I loved the work I did with him. I loved the way he was. I loved being the assistant crack-pot. I loved his house—my house. What does that mean, "put my brain in a cage"? Did I love my uncle because I loved art? Or was it his knowledge that deceived me, or that … Or what?

I woke up again, without having felt that I had fallen asleep, with the end of a sentence in my head: " … and who is not even capable of living with a woman, not even interesting enough for her to want to love me for more than six weeks".

I stood up and walked through the carriages until I reached the bar. I ordered a beer. I was handed an aluminium can.

I drank it and found it insipid. That was only natural after the Munich one. Tasteless. Worthless. Like me.

At the Gare de l'Est, I recovered my car and did my best through the Parisian congestion to regain the quiet confines of Brie, where Uncle Charles had chosen to settle in this old house, austere like the dignified people of private means who had erected it in the past in their own image and which he gradually toned down, without removing its severity, with the help of books, odds and ends, paintings and, perhaps, his smile.

I was never one to drive very fast on the roads. This road was an exception. The last kilometres, the final turnings around the fields and groves, I knew them by heart. They seemed interminable, in my haste to be back in that home, that resting place (how those words seem apt ...), that I continued to call my uncle's house, although it was now mine and had been so for five years, through inheritance. But an inheritance is an inheritance. The person one inherits from remains the proprietor. It is he who is present. This house, my house, so much too big for me, remains my uncle's house. I was only the heir. Heir of what? A house, some paintings, beautiful furniture, thousands of books, thousands of pages, the labour of a lifetime. *What did I do with my life?* uncle wrote in his notebook. I recalled those words as I was driving, from turning to turning, from village to hamlet. A lifetime of work, all of that to finally write: *What did I do with my life?* Poor uncle. Did I inherit that too? A lifetime of work, and then: *For one month I had the passion for painting.* Him, one month. Me, six weeks? What is a woman in one's life? One month, six weeks. Since the mouthful of tasteless beer in the train bar, I hadn't stopped rolling around in my head bits of sentences, ones I would never have imagined hearing in Uncle Charles' mouth, and that I had read however, written by his prudent and scrupulous hand. *It is to begin to love no longer. I had the passion for painting for one month.*

When I left the road, I still had that long straight dirt track lined by small elms that people used to like in the nineteenth century and right at the end, in its perspective, I could see my uncle's house, I mean, my house. Not once did I drive those last five hundred metres without some kind of joy. That straight line, that procession of small round trees, on the right and left, with the noble and simple façade at its end, made of old bricks, old stones, old tiles, yes, I know, one could be accused of being retrograde, obscurantist, outside of life, outside the run of things, against progress, attached to the past. I resisted, this time, the temptation of a litany of adjectives ending in 'ist', asking instead: Why should I fight happiness at all costs?

I didn't see it straightaway. At the end of the avenue, at the bottom of the flight of steps, framed by the perspective of the elms, there right at the back, by the flowering rhododendrons, I could see the Citroën, round and green like a firm cabbage.

Would I ever become accustomed to any of the dramas conceived, planned, ordered and arranged by Sarah? No, I knew that. She made use of every conceivable accessory, even those of chance, passing time, fatigue, solitude and emptiness. She used them to amplify the contrasts and double their impacts. I knew that. Yes, I knew that. I jammed the brakes much too hard. The car skidded on the gravel with a sound like an avalanche. Sarah was already coming out to the terrace before I had time to climb the steps. She looked at me and started to laugh when I stumbled, missed a step. It was a timid laugh that I saw on her lips rather than heard. We didn't say a word, not even hello. She clung to me, or me to her, I don't recall. I put my hand on her neck and caressed her hair. We remained that way for a long time without moving. I looked behind her at the open door, then closed my eyes, without thinking. What a capacity for emptiness I'd acquired in those few days. She was first to speak, in a voice I didn't recognize: shy, almost trembling, a murmur.

"Pierre … "

"Hush," I whispered and stroked her neck and soft hair. She let me caress her, then took my other hand and placed it on her belly.

"Pierre, I'm pregnant."

Never ever, not once, have I anticipated, not even for a split second, what Sarah would say. Never have I foreseen, guessed, outrun or been ready on time. Sarah's surprises were always fast, nervous, sharp. They burst like cinders, crackled for a second, then flicked away in a fleeting cascade of laughter. This had to be the surprise of all surprises: the one that slid across my chest with the breeze of her whisper, threaded its way between the stitches of my pullover and white scarf, penetrated me silently, like a mouse.

I stroked her hair. She didn't move. Her cheek against my chest, she held my hand on her belly. I concluded by saying, under my breath:

"Good God, Sarah … Did we do that?"

I don't know exactly what I meant to say. I was talking in a daze. As soon as I had spoken, something like embarrassment crept over my stupor. I was afraid not to say what needed to be said or that she wouldn't understand what I was going to say, that my bewilderment would lead her to believe that … that what? I breathed:

"Are you happy?"

And I sank back into my black hole, thinking I'd made another blunder.

She didn't answer. At least not with words. Her hands

began to move mine in a spiral, and she started to stroke her belly with my hand.

I live by repeating litanies. Confusion, unexpected emotion, disarray filled my brain with cotton wool and, in the haze, I recite.

I recited: "We did that?" My sentence meandered tortuously and silently, hiding in moss and dead leaves. We kept quiet. I felt Sarah's head turning over against my chest. Left cheek. Right cheek. The hand which caressed her neck was now on her lips. She whispered on my hand:

"We'll call him Charles, if we really must."

I guessed a long time before that Sarah possessed a kind of genius, but I hadn't really measured it before this minute, this second. Not only did she guess what one thought, but she guessed what one hadn't even managed to think yet. When one thought she was skipping from one subject to the next, it was simply because she pressed on and asked a question that followed from the answer to a question one hadn't yet posed. I was turning in my head the "we did that?" without even understanding what it really meant. And she, not knowing anything about what I knew, was already thinking for me: "What Uncle Charles messed up, we have succeeded in doing."

I almost trembled. I don't know if, after a few seconds, I would have found enough calm to open my mouth and say something, I don't know what, with words. She didn't leave me the time. Without moving her head, without moving her lips from beneath my hand, she said, with a little tremor of joy in her voice:

"But swear, you have to swear, that when you see him for the first time in his cot, you're not going to say that he resembles Van Eyck's baby Jesus in the Louvre Museum."

I knew that baby Jesus. She had placed him as background

(that was her word) on her computer. He appeared as soon as she turned it on. He was the cutest, the cheekiest, the funniest of all the baby Jesuses that had ever been painted. He was not by Van Eyck, but Van der Weyden. He was not in the Louvre, but in Bruges. It didn't matter.

I answered into her hair.

"Promise."